Sherlock Holmes and the Hearthstone Manuscript

As Edited By

Daniel D. Victor, Ph.D.

Book Ten in the Series,
Sherlock Holmes and the American Literati

First edition published in 2024
© Copyright 2024
Daniel Victor

The right of Daniel Victor to be identified as the author of this work has been asserted by him in accordance with the Copyright, Designs and Patents Act 1998.

All rights reserved. No reproduction, copy or transmission of this publication may be made without express prior written permission. No paragraph of this publication may be reproduced, copied or transmitted except with express prior written permission or in accordance with the provisions of the Copyright Act 1956 (as amended). Any person who commits any unauthorised act in relation to this publication may be liable to criminal prosecution and civil claims for damage.

All characters appearing in this work are fictitious. Any resemblance to real persons, living or dead, is purely coincidental. The opinions expressed herein are those of the author and not of MX Publishing.

Hardcover 978-1-80424-461-6
Paperback ISBN 978-1-80424-462-3
ePub ISBN 978-1-80424-463-0
PDF ISBN 978-1-80424-464-7

Published by MX Publishing
335 Princess Park Manor, Royal Drive,
London, N11 3GX
www.mxpublishing.co.uk

Cover design Brian Belanger

Also by Daniel D. Victor

Cruel September

The Seventh Bullet:
The Further Adventures of Sherlock Holmes

A Study in Synchronicity

Sherlock Holmes and the Shadows of
St Petersburg

The Literary Adventures of Sherlock Holmes,
Volumes 1 and 2

Other Books in the Series,
"Sherlock Holmes and the American Literati":

The Final Page of Baker Street

Sherlock Holmes and the
Baron of Brede Place

Seventeen Minutes to Baker Street

The Outrage at the Diogenes Club

Sherlock Holmes and the London Particular

The Astounding Murder at Cloverwood House

Sherlock Holmes and the Pandemic of Death

Sherlock Holmes and the Case of the Fateful Arrow

Sherlock Holmes and a Tale of Greed

Acknowledgments

Many thanks to Tom Turley for his constant encouragement and to Seth Victor and Ethan Victor, to whom I always turn with questions about baseball. Much appreciation also to Sandy Cohen, an indefatigable source of support. Additional thanks to Judy Grabiner, a most insightful reader, who raises all the right questions. And, of course, my deepest appreciation and love to my wife, Norma Silverman, who never seems to tire of helping me refine Dr. Watson's narratives.

A note on the text:
All headnotes, footnotes, and chapter titles were added to Dr. Watson's manuscript by the editor.

When the high road nearly reached the summit
it was carried in a curve along the edge of a strange
depression, a vast basin in the sand-hills, sinking three
hundred feet to a marshy bottom full of oozing springs.
This is termed the Devil's Punch Bowl.
— Sabine Baring-Gould
The Broom-Squire

The grass on which they stood, had once been dyed with gore;
and the blood of the murdered man had run down, drop by
drop, into the hollow which gives the place its name.
"The Devil's Bowl," thought Nicholas, as he looked into the
void, "never held fitter liquor than that!"
— Charles Dickens
*The Life and Adventures
of Nicholas Nickleby*

A Pair of Letters

[From Sherlock Holmes to Mrs. Mary Isabel Garland Lord]

                                        Sussex
                            22 March 1940

My Dear Mrs. Lord,

    Please accept my condolences on the recent death of your father. Though decades have passed since I first met Hamlin Garland, I still recall how instrumental was his role in a murder investigation in which my colleague, the late Dr John Watson, and I participated.

In point of fact, your father's dedication to solving the crime in question has encouraged me to send you the accompanying manuscript that documents the investigation. As you might expect, the text was compiled a number of years ago by my dear friend, Watson. Unfortunately, he never got round to giving it a title, and based on where most of the events in the account take place, I simply refer to it as "The Hearthstone Manuscript." Ever intent on sharing it with you, I have kept it in my villa here on the South Downs rather than including it with Watson's other unpublished sketches, which remain in London in his dispatch box in the vault of Cox and Co., Charing Cross.

Especially appealing to you, I should imagine, is that the part of your father's diary that he shared with us comprises almost a third of Watson's manuscript. I knew your father as a humble man, who would never have taken it upon himself to advertise his heroic exploits — particularly in a story based on the heated passions and violent actions that so distressed him. It was, in fact, your father's discomfort with such matters, not to mention his distaste for crime stories, that convinced Watson all those years ago not to publish the account.

Good old Watson! Considerate to a fault. As I am certain he would have approved, I have followed his lead in this matter and waited until your father's passing before sharing Watson's account with you. One can only hope that in your time of grief, reading it will provide you a degree of solace.

I would, of course, have preferred presenting the manuscript to you in person, but as the ghastly war with Germany continues, I find most all of my time consumed with little else. I trust you understand how the idea of leaving my homeland during this dangerous period remains utterly incomprehensible.

Yours sincerely,

S. Holmes

[From Isabel Garland to Sherlock Holmes]

Hollywood, California
May 15, 1940

Dear Mr. Holmes,

I can't thank you enough for your kind words. I really miss Daddy and the glorious times we spent together, especially when I was his little Mary Isabel and he was my Poppie. Needless to say, I am also particularly grateful to receive Dr. Watson's manuscript. Like my father, I too have followed your adventures through the writings of your friend, and I read the narrative that you sent me as soon as it arrived.

I must say that Dr. Watson was quite right in not publishing the account during Daddy's lifetime. As you have correctly noted, Daddy was more than a bit strait-laced on topics like violence and crime. Though he called himself a "fictionist," an author who documented human behavior in his writings, Daddy had his limits.

Rather than expanding the role of literature as he assumed all fiction should do, Daddy believed that sensational tales about the passions, are written solely to fill the coffers of magazine- and book-publishers. "Daughtie," he would say to me, "those stories should be considered nothing more than pornography." Ironic, really, that a man who cultivated so rebellious a voice in defense of the poor farmer could not strike a similar note in defense of more open-minded writers.*

Personally, I had no idea that Daddy was involved in helping solve a terrible crime, let alone playing so heroic a role in the solution. He certainly never told my sister, Connie, or me about it, and Mother used to say that he wasn't beyond removing pages from his diary or changing the chronological order of events to suit his purpose.

All that being said, however, I think that the events described by Dr. Watson are so dramatic that they deserve to be retold. Furthermore, as Hamlin Garland's older daughter, I believe that I should be the one to retell them. Despite his prudish dislike of crime stories, I feel confident that he would have approved of my plan.

You see, at bottom Daddy didn't totally oppose such stories. On some occasion or other, he confessed to us that when he was a boy, he liked to read penny-dreadfuls, especially the adventures of the Old Sleuth or Captain Jack Harkaway. In his later years, he came to enjoy the crime stories of Edgar Wallace. He even prodded me to begin the murder mystery set in Hollywood that I had thought about writing in my youth.

Despite Daddy's mellowing on the subject, I still plan to honor his desire for privacy.

---

* A sarcastic Sinclair Lewis, who considered such hypocrisy typically American, decided that Garland's inconsistency logically qualified him to be viewed as "the dean of American letters."

To that end, I intend to fictionalize the plot of Dr. Watson's manuscript and disguise the identities of the people involved. I've also decided to set the story in America rather than in England. Should anyone ask, I'll say that the idea for writing the book came from "out of the blue."

As you may know, my husband, Mendrit Lord, is himself the author of numerous "whodunits" and radio dramas. When I told him I hoped to fabricate the details of a real-life murder mystery, my dear husband said he was eager to offer guidance. Who knows? If all goes well with this book (which I'm thinking of titling Abandon Hope), Mendrit and I may work together on additional mysteries. Perhaps, we might even create a scene or two that celebrate you, Mr. Holmes.*·

Again, I thank you for your condolences. Since so much of your own relationship with Dr. Watson appears through his narratives, I can well appreciate how his passing must enable you to sympathize with my personal loss. The opportunity you have given me to honor my father is truly wonderful. I am deeply moved by your kindness.

And, please, do keep yourself safe from Mr. Hitler.

---

* Following the 1941 publication of Isabel's *Abandon Hope*, she and Mendrit wrote four novels together under the name of Garland Lord: *Murder's Little Helper* (1941), which includes the line, "Look, dear, you're playing Sherlock Holmes tonight—not Cleopatra"; *She Never Grew Old* (1942); *Murder with Love* (1943); and *Murder Plain and Fancy* (1943).

With deep appreciation,

Isabel Garland Lord

Isabel Garland Lord

Postscript:
I should also mention seeing William Gillette play you on stage in a production that Daddy took me to — the tickets were given to him by Mr. Gillette himself. Our trip to the theater was compensation for my having apologized to my father in a situation in which he was definitely in the wrong; Mother maintained that Daddy was never very good at saying he was sorry.

The Hearthstone Manuscript

By

John H. Watson, M.D.

Chapter One

Our American Visitor

> I devoured *Jack Harkaway* and *The Quaker Sleuth*
> precisely as I played ball—to pass the time
> and because I enjoyed the game.
> —Hamlin Garland
> *A Son of the Middle Border*

"Watson," Sherlock Holmes glared at me, "kindly recall that Mr. Garland is here to report a possible murder."

"There's plenty of time for that, Holmes," said I, holding up my hand. "Let him first tell us about his passion for sport."

Rare was the occasion that Sherlock Holmes and I disagreed in front of a client. But such was indeed the case that memorable spring day in 1899. I for one hoped to learn more about the intricacies of American baseball from the brown-bearded author from the States who stood before us. Hamlin Garland had just returned to London after visiting some well-known personages in Surrey, including my literary agent, Arthur Conan Doyle, a man—it must be said—who fancied himself a baseball enthusiast.

Yet Holmes had little use for Garland's posturing at the centre of our room to illustrate the meeting with Conan Doyle. After all, besides the alleged murder that Garland said had brought him to Baker Street in the first place, there were more important matters in the world than sport with which to concern oneself. What of the escalating differences between the British and the Boers in South Africa or the battles America was fighting with revolutionaries in the Philippines?

Still, one could see a purpose in encouraging Garland to talk about his favourite diversion. At the very least, it might serve to brighten his demeanour. The author presented a gruff and deprecatory attitude despite the thousands in royalties he had reportedly received from Macmillans for his recently-published *Main Traveled Roads*, an account of the hopelessness of rural life in Midwestern America.

Why, after only little more than a week in our fair city, he complained that London, the centre of the greatest empire in the world, had not lived up to his expectations. "Not toweringly impressive" was the way he described it. In his clear, high-pitched voice, he faulted the yellow pall that overhung the buildings, the ugly omnibuses clogging the streets, and the dingy and dark atmosphere that seemed to permeate every corner.

At first, I was distinctly put off by his negative point of view, but I soon came to realise that it was not London itself that had so distressed Garland, but rather cities in general. To Hamlin Garland, London merely served as a surrogate for any city in which he might find himself. It was life in the country that he seemed to miss, and he had a difficult time concealing his melancholy.

Yet when he talked about baseball, whose playing fields offered the verdant and earthy hues of a bucolic landscape, his attitude changed. His voice, dropping to a rich baritone, took on a musical cadence. He was, I knew, a successful public orator and understood how to maintain an audience's attention. To that end, I kicked aside the bearskin hearthrug to provide him the space to further dramatize his account.

For his part, Sherlock Holmes picked up a copy of *The Times* and positioned himself behind its pages.

Even as Hamlin Garland stood with his back to me, an imaginary baseball in hand, I could sense the energy that marked his spirit. In that respect, the forty-year-old author seemed like a child.

Stretching to his full six-foot height, he spoke over his shoulder. "Doyle and I tossed a ball around in '94 when I first met him in America." Turning slightly, he cradled the imaginary ball at the middle of his chest a few inches below his beard. With his thick, brown hair combed straight back, his feet together, and his muscular arms readily apparent in his white shirtsleeves, Garland presented quite the athletic frame, a physique he attributed to the years spent labouring so strenuously on his father's farms.

"When I saw Doyle this time," Garland said, "he hoped to learn about the science of pitching. He wanted information about the break of our 'inshoots' and 'outdrops,'* not to mention—I love the way he put it— the pitcher's ability to confound the laws of astronomy by making a sphere alter its course in mid-air."

"Watson," Holmes growled, "was not one baseballer this year enough for you?"

I knew Holmes was referring to Stephen Crane, another American writer whom we had met a few months before. Crane had played the positions of catcher and shortstop in college, and like Conan Doyle, Crane too had tossed a ball with the very same Hamlin Garland.

"Even though the sky was darkening," Garland continued, "Doyle led me out to his tennis court. We played only a single set when he realised that there was enough room for me to demonstrate

---

* According to *The Dickson Baseball Dictionary*, in nineteenth-century baseball terminology, an "inshoot" is a fast pitch or "swift" that "breaks... toward the batter, but not as sharp as a curve." An "outdrop" is a curve ball that "drops down as it approaches the batter" instead of breaking away or "out" like an "outcurve."

inner and outer curves. So he handed me a cherry-red cricket ball and asked to watch me throw.

"I've pitched a bit, you know, and hefting the cricket ball in my palm, I told him I'd feel more comfortable throwing an actual baseball. Doyle threw back his head and laughed. 'There probably isn't such a thing in all of England,' he proclaimed."

"Quite so," muttered Sherlock Holmes, not bothering to look up from his copy of the *Times*.

I, on the other hand, wished to hear more of what the American had to say about the game he loved. His crime report could wait a bit. After all, how nefarious a transgression could it be if he was not even certain that a crime had actually been committed?

On the subject of pitching, however, the American was more precise. "The leather cricket ball Doyle had given me was smaller and heavier than a baseball," he explained, "and thus more difficult to control. Still, I had no other choice, so I rubbed my hands all over it to get a feel for the thing—its stitching, its ridges, its roughness. So impressed was Doyle at my handling of the ball that he told me I could keep it as a souvenir. In fact, it's in my valise if you want to see it." He nodded in the direction of the small suitcase he had left near the door.

I held up a hand. "No need," I said boastfully. "I know cricket balls. I played when I was a child. I'm aware that they're harder than baseballs, and yet is it not the case that American players feel it necessary to wear leather gloves to protect their hands? A bit faint-hearted, if you ask me."

"That's true, Watson," Garland said, "and Doyle felt the same. To get used to the cricket ball, I wanted to make a few practice throws, and true to the British tradition, he claimed no need for a glove—not that he needed one for those early tosses."

"Hmph," Holmes grunted from behind his paper.

"What happened next?" the sportsman in me persisted.

"Well, I marked off the appropriate distance—sixty feet, six inches. Back in '93," he said, seemingly proud of his arcane knowledge, "they added five feet to the distance—and then—" here he strode forward with one leg and "winding up" (as the Americans call it), he announced, "I threw him the pill." At the same time, he spoke the words, he raised both hands above his head and then whipped his right arm downward in a sweeping, circular motion.

Garland paused to take a breath. "I must tell you, Watson, I didn't hold back, and Doyle—still gloveless—didn't complain. I launched a variety of curves at him for half an hour, and with just a wince or two, he caught them all bare-handed—that is, until I let fly my swift ball. For that one, he had the good sense to step aside. 'This demonstration is now over,' he declared."

"Ever practical," I observed, "that's Conan Doyle for you."

"Enough!" shouted Sherlock Holmes, flinging down the newspaper. "Unless I heard incorrectly, Garland, you said you'd come here to report a death at the place you were visiting—a 'suspicious death,' I believe you called it. Can you not now tell us about this possible crime instead of how to toss—what did you call it?—a 'pill'?"

"You're right, Holmes," Garland replied. "What was I thinking?" He took a deep breath and donning his frock coat, stroked his brown beard, and resumed his chair. As he turned from the topic of baseball to the speculation of murder, I could not help noticing how the fire that had lit up his deep-set eyes seemed to diminish a bit.

Chapter Two

Hamlin Garland's Story

> . . . I had often seen a tennis ball, struck with an oblique racket, describe such a curve line. For, a circular as well as a progressive motion being communicated to it by a stroke, its parts on that side, where the motions conspire, must press and beat the contiguous air more violently than on the other, and there excite a reluctancy and reaction of the air proportionably greater.
> —Isaac Newton
> *Philosophical Transactions
> of the Royal Society of London*
> 19 February, 1671/72

"Let me begin by explaining why I've come here this afternoon," said Hamlin Garland.

"At last," muttered Holmes.

"You see, gentlemen, during our various conversations, Doyle told me that if ever you have a mystery to solve, there's no better man for the job than Sherlock Holmes. He called you 'the world's first consulting detective,' Holmes, and he spoke the words so proudly, you might have thought he composed the title himself."

Holmes, always the appreciator of compliments—especially when they come from a figure with the social standing of someone like Arthur Conan Doyle—allowed himself the briefest of smiles.

"Who died?" I asked.

"And what made the death so suspicious?" Holmes followed.

Garland pointed at me. "Your question first, Watson. The person who died is a woman named Muriel Laughton Cobb. She is—was—the mother of a friend I'd come to England to visit—the English poet, Owen Lester Cobb."

"I don't know the name," said Holmes.

"Nor do I," I added.

"Sad but true," Garland agreed. "That's part of the problem. I first met Owen in Chicago. At his wedding actually. He'd come to America to make a name for himself and ended up marrying a friend of Zulime Taft, the girl I'd been courting. As it turned out, however, apart from appearing in a few little-known journals, Owen's poetry wasn't catching on in the States—to be honest, he's admitted that it hasn't done any better over here—and though he comes from a wealthy English family, he was running low on funds."

"A perennial problem for poets," I observed.

"For many a writer," said Garland. "Believe me, I know. In any case, Owen asked his mother for help, but rather than sending him money, she offered him the job of overseeing Hearthstone Hall, the family estate in Surrey. At the very least, accepting the position would provide free room and board for him and his wife, Lucille.

"'I don't want to go back home,' he told me, 'not with a new bride. It feels so infantile.'

"Still, with no practical alternatives, Owen had to accept his mother's offer. But not, I should add, before extending me an invitation to come visit Lucille and him here in England."

"Most generous," I said.

"Well, not long thereafter, I heard from Zulime's brother—Lorado Taft, the sculptor—that the lady I had been spending all my time with—that is, his sister—was already engaged to someone else. I knew nothing about such a circumstance. To be sure, she was a challenge to win over; but even so, I couldn't believe she could treat me in such a two-faced manner.

"I was so incensed that I immediately decided to leave town. I've always wanted to see the world, and—well—here was an opportunity for me, a literary man to my bones, to visit the land of Chaucer and Shakespeare—not to mention the invitations I'd gotten in the past few years from writers like Bernard Shaw and Doyle in Surrey and Henry James in Rye. Nor could I forget my most recent invitation from Owen. In a word, I decided to come to England."

"At last," sighed Sherlock Holmes, "the story moves forward." He retired to the mantel where he reached for the Persian slipper in which he kept his shag. After filling his briar and striking a vesta, he drew on his pipe and returned to his chair.

I offered Garland one of the cigars we kept in the coal scuttle, but he waved it off.

"When did you arrive in England?" Holmes asked.

"I got to Liverpool on Wednesday, April 26, and to London the day after. That's when I telegraphed Owen and Lucille. You see, no less a figure than George Bernard Shaw, with whom I'd previously corresponded, had invited me to Blen Cathra, his home in Hindhead, for a night in early May. Since Dr. Doyle was nearby, I hoped to combine my visits.

"I told Owen that I'd be visiting people in Surrey in a week or so—and he suggested that I come for dinner, at Hearthstone, which was also in Hindhead, at seven o'clock this past Saturday. Which I did."

"Hindhead," I mused. I knew of the small literary community in Surrey, of course. It included Conan Doyle, as well as Bernard Shaw, the witty Irish dramatist; Grant Allen, the Canadian novelist; and Hettie Huxley, the widow of biologist T. H. Huxley. Of poet Owen Lester Cobb and Hearthstone

Hall, however, I confess to having heard nothing at all.

"I sailed on the *Teutonic* from New York on the nineteenth of April," Garland continued. "I must admit that almost immediately I began to feel queer, and I spent virtually all of the voyage in my bunk in a cabin not much bigger than a coffin. I got to Liverpool at the end of a miserable week. The ship's doctor said he'd not seen a worse case of seasickness in his thirty years' experience."

"My sympathy," I offered whilst Holmes puffed sedately on his pipe,

Garland shrugged. "Can't say it didn't prepare me for the rigours of London."

"Here now," I said, preparing to defend the metropolis, "you can't—"

But Garland simply ploughed on. "In Liverpool I managed to board one of your quaint Midland Expresses, and through the green and empty countryside it conveyed me here to this city so full of people. I secured a room in a little hotel called Edwards House near Euston Station. The place was a bit primitive, but then just about everything I've come across here in London feels that way."

"Now see here—" I retorted, but this time Garland put up his hands to quiet me.

"Come now, Doctor," he said, "modern London is about as ugly as Chicago—although I must say that Chicago's sidewalks are wider and its buildings are taller."

I remained silent whilst Holmes continued to puff on his pipe.

"Historic London is different," Garland conceded. "I'll give you that. In fact, I spent my first week here being quite impressed by the traditional sights—Piccadilly Circus, Trafalgar Square, the Houses of Parliament, the Tower, the Law Courts.

"What's more, I also had time to shop. You see, the British writer Israel Zangwill, whom I'd last seen in New York, had convinced me that my traditional frock coat"—he plucked at his sleeves—"is sadly out of date."

"Holmes and I both know Zangwill," I told Garland. "Conan Doyle introduced us. Zangwill's a principled fellow whose advice may be safely followed."

Garland nodded. "Good—because I believed him when he told me that if I hoped to be welcomed into English literary circles, I needed a swallow-tail coat. I'd always viewed the claw-hammer suit as the livery of privilege, but Zangwill seemed to have my best interest at heart, so I let him steer me towards some traditional English clothes. He helped me find a white tie, high collars, linen, and gloves to go along with the swallow-tail. He said it was time to tame the cowboy."

"And what, pray, does all this have to do with a murder?" Holmes wanted to know.

"I'm getting to that," Garland said, "but I want you to know that I carried with me the correct clothes when I took the train to Haslemere."

"Right," I said, "the stop closest to Hindhead. I've made the journey myself many times."

"I tell you, gentlemen, I felt duly important upon my arrival. Shaw had sent a horse-drawn cart—a trap, I guess you call it—with a driver in brown uniform to meet me at the station. I must confess that I don't have the money for a long stay in England, so to budget my time I spent just a day and night at Blen Cathra. Quite a fellow, that Shaw. No swallow-tails required there, I assure you."

"The murder you spoke of?" demanded Holmes, his teeth clenched on the pipe stem.

"Right, I'm getting there. Well, Mr. Shaw was kind enough to have his man drive me on to Undershaw, Doyle's home. The place is most impressive—all those gables, that red-brick and white trim. Even stained-glass windows."

"Yes, yes," mumbled my friend.

"I spent most of Thursday at Undershaw," said Garland. "I like Doyle. He's a hearty fellow. He, his wife, and I had a marvellous mid-day meal of cold salmon. Afterwards, while out on the tennis court, as I've already explained—"

"In great detail," Holmes confirmed dryly.

"—the doctor and I resumed our discussion about baseball from years before."

Holmes exhaled a great cloud of thick smoke, a warning signal that Garland was verging off the topic again.

"I understand your concerns, Holmes," said the American. "You want to know about the death at Hearthstone and why I called it 'suspicious.' As I've already said, explaining all that is why I've come here. But I'm a professional story-teller, and I must tell a story at my own pace. My father trained me. As a farmer, you know, he was both vivid and concise."

"Concise?" Holmes repeated sceptically, but motioned for Garland to continue.

"Doyle offered to have his man drive me the few miles to Hearthstone Hall, a ride I'll not soon forget, I tell you, gentlemen. That excursion in Doyle's trap was like travelling into another world. The house stands by itself on a rocky precipice overlooking what the locals call 'The Devil's Punch Bowl.'"

Both Holmes and I know the area. One cannot avoid viewing it whilst visiting Conan Doyle. Surrounded chiefly by pines, the so-called bowl is a seven-hundred-acre, ravine-like depression some three-hundred feet deep.

Though quite beautiful on sunny days, much of the time the irregular terrain and gorse-covered ridges look inhospitable—foreboding, one might say. Indeed, much of the stark countryside puts me in mind of the bleak landscape near Baskerville Hall in Dartmoor, where the so-called "hound from hell" once roamed.

No one would ever mistake the scenic countryside of Surrey for the menacing moorland of Devonshire with its fantastical tors and overhanging crags—not to mention the local fear of legendary beasts. But one cannot deny a disturbing similarity between the sloping sand-hills and pooling marshes of the Punch Bowl and the rugged hillocks and boggy swampland of Dartmoor's Grimpen Mire. I confess in these pages that on not a few occasions, I found myself embellishing my own descriptions of the Devonshire landscape with some dramatic views I appropriated whilst skirting the uninviting hollow near Hindhead.

"Conan Doyle's coachman," reported Garland, "was quick to inform me of the terrors of the place. The fellow brought the trap to a stop and pointed downward into the ravine with his whip. ''Tis said demons dwell there, sir. 'Tis a place where the ancients believed that Satan 'imself dug up clods of earth to cast up at 'eaven in his war against the gods. 'Tis a bottomless pit, sir,' he said with another shake of his whip. 'a true 'ellscape,' you might call it."

"Superstitious claptrap," I offered.

Garland readily agreed. "And yet, I could understand the man's anxiety," he said. "The Punch Bowl looks eerily like the small Wisconsin valley where I spent the first eight years of my life. Green's Coulee, it's called, and it's less than a quarter the size, but it used to frighten me just as much as I imagine the Punch Bowl frightens people who frequent it today." *

"If all the local gossip is to be believed," I said.

"When I was little," Garland recalled, "there was lots to be afraid of. I feared the red men who lived beyond our rim, the monsters that might climb their way out of the marsh, or the swamps themselves where the thick mud might suck you down forever. And that's not to mention the snakes. Back then, people called them 'serpents'—like in the Bible. To us children, 'serpents' sounded more devil-like than 'snakes.' In Green's Coulee, every path held a terror; every swale, some sort of nightmare.

"Of course, I was only four years old at the time and didn't know any better. When I returned to the coulee as a young man, I could appreciate its beauty, especially during those bucolic sunsets when

---

* Perhaps, it was the vivid descriptions of the same Devil's Punch Bowl in Edgar Wallace's novel, *The Man from Morocco*, that helped Hamlin Garland come to appreciate Wallace's crime stories—as reported by Isabel Garland Lord in her letter to Sherlock Holmes included before the start of Watson's narrative.

the hills were tinged with gold. Search any city—New York, Chicago, London—and try as you might, you will never find a scene more beautiful, more magical, than a sunset out in the wild country. Why, my own mother, now in her later years and decades removed from the Coulee, wishes that the family had never left.

"As for the coachman, he snapped the reins at his high-stepping horse to get the creature moving again. 'Don't like to stay too long,' he said. 'There was that murder what occurred 'ere many years ago. A sailor was robbed and killed down there—'ad his 'ead cut almost clean off, 'e did. That's enough to keep me away.'"

Holmes pointed the stem of his pipe at Garland. "The infamous murder which your driver referenced occurred in the last century. You may rest assured that the region's infamous appellation, 'The Devil's Punchbowl,' predates the crime."

"Whenever the murder," offered Garland, "the whole area has a sombre look; it's barren and strange at the same time. With the woodland shrouding the slopes the way it does, I imagine that even on the sunniest of days much of the landscape remains in shadows, especially the morass at the bottom. To make it worse, this past Saturday, dark clouds filled the heavens. I figured that my broad-brimmed sombrero would more likely serve to protect me from the rain than from any rays of a non-existent sun.

"Soon we entered a road lined with beech trees on both sides. The canopy formed by their branches made the scene even darker. Worse, the road grew narrower as we climbed—an inauspicious approach to a house that Owen had described as being large as a hotel.

"Actually, thanks to the thick fog that was by then blanketing much of the gorse- and heather-covered hillsides, it was only when we were almost on top of the place that I finally saw it, a squat, grey structure encircled by a first-floor balcony. I tell you, gentlemen, its two half-shaded windows set to the left and right of the oaken front door put me in mind of the hooded eyes and gaping maw of some great creature."

Sherlock Holmes raised a critical eyebrow. "Will no one spare me from theatrical writers?" he muttered and exhaled another cloud of smoke.

Chapter Three

Hearthstone Hall

> What is essential is that here is a splendid game which calls for a fine eye, activity, bodily fitness, and judgment in the highest degree.
> —Arthur Conan Doyle
> "Merits of Baseball"
> Letter to *The Times*
> 28 October 1924

"As the cart crunched onto the gravel in front of Hearthstone Hall Saturday night, I realised it was near eight o'clock and I was an hour late for dinner. A muscular, red-headed fellow in greasy grey-canvas overalls came running out to attend to the trap-horse. He would have fit right into that league of red-heads you gentlemen investigated a few years ago."

"Jabez Wilson," I remembered from the curious case.

"Well, this fellow's named Fairley—or so I learned later—and as soon as he took hold of the bridle, the horse reared its head and snorted. In return, Fairley spat upon the gravel.

"Turns out that Fairley's the gamekeeper at Hearthstone. They keep a few horses, swine, and chickens there. I did the same kind of work on my father's farms, and the man has my sympathy."

Holmes continued to draw on his pipe, remaining silent for this part of Garland's account.

"I could only hope that my late arrival would cause no problems, yet as soon as the trap had pulled up, the front door opened and there emerged an older woman, her grey hair pulled tightly back into a knot. Dressed in black and standing tall, she did nothing more than observe, but her furrowed brow and the severe straight line of her dark eyebrows indicated the displeasure she experienced at my lateness.

"Ordinarily, gentlemen, I get along well with women of that age. I suppose I see my aging mother in them. But in this case, so uninviting did she appear that I almost instructed Doyle's coachman to take me back to Undershaw.

"Only the appearance of my friend, Owen, caused me to change my mind. He came bounding out of the house past the scowling lady and approached the trap to welcome me. His stringy black hair was longer than I remembered, but his smile was just as broad as it had been back in Chicago.

"'Garland,' he shouted, 'so glad to see you.'

"'Sorry if I'm late,' I said as I climbed down from my seat.

"'Not to worry, old fellow,' he replied.

"Grabbing my valise, I signalled good-bye to the driver. 'Be careful in the fog,' I told him, and he reassured me that I need not worry.

"'I know the lie of the land,' he said, adding that as Doyle had instructed, he would come back Monday morning to convey me to the Haslemere train station so I could return to London. A train was leaving just past eight for Waterloo.

"Fairley let go of the reins, gave the departing horse a swat on its flank, and spat onto the gravel once more. I watched the trap disappear into the fog, and then I looked about for Lucille.

"'Where's your bride?' I asked my friend.

"Immediately, Owen's smile faded. With the flick of his head, he indicated the woman at the door. 'My mother,' he said."

"Aha!" exclaimed Holmes. "The alleged murder victim herself."

"Right you are. Though obviously none of this was known to me at the time. In any case, Owen explained that with dinner delayed, his mother had put Lucille to work.

"'Mother has her dusting the house,' he told me. 'I'm afraid that my wife has yet to accept the routine. You see, Mater places great faith in the maxim, 'Idleness is the devil's workshop. Come, let me introduce you.'

"As I approached the steps to the front porch, I could see the woman looking me over and cocking a critical eyebrow at what she saw. Take your pick, gentlemen. My imitation-leather valise? My shiny, black frock coat? My travel-worn, wide-brimmed hat? Or maybe it was simply my casual American style that she didn't approve of. The more I thought about it, however, the more I believed her attitude might just as easily have been based on upper-class snobbery."

Familiar socialist blather, I thought and, judging from what Garland had said before about poor farmers, not all that surprising.

Nor was he finished. "I know such highbrows back home. Owning grand houses like Hearthstone enables them to look down upon the rest of us. I described the sort in *Main Traveled Roads*— the conservative business types who farmed the farmers, who inflicted their ugliness on the lives of the hardworking poor. I can assure you, gentlemen, that by revealing in my writings the hypocrisy of the rich, I have earned the enmity of the ruling classes."

"A bit harsh, wouldn't you say, Garland?" enquired Holmes. "If, as you have suggested, a woman of the ruling-class was murdered, you don't want to furnish cause to implicate yourself."

"Agreed," he shrugged. "After all, Mrs. Cobb was not only my hostess but also my friend's mother. I simply tipped my sombrero and held out my hand. She gripped it firmly and, if a bit coldly, welcomed me to her home.

"'Sorry,' I said to her, assuming—mistakenly, as I would quickly learn—that my politesse might curry favour. 'Sorry for being late.'

"'Let us adjourn to the dinner table, Mr. Garland,' the woman said, 'and hope that tonight's fare has not been rendered overdone by your tardiness. Charity Bookman, our cook, can work wonders in the kitchen, but—as I'm certain you will agree—misspent time is an enemy of the perfect meal.'"

One could only shake one's head at the unpleasant reception Garland had described. "Not the most agreeable of welcomes, I must say."

"I tell you, gentlemen," Garland confessed, "I felt put in my place. Still, I had no choice but to follow the woman inside.

"What can I say? The place was oppressive. It lacked light, and ponderous furniture loomed everywhere. Antique paintings of frowning men hung on the walls; heavy drapes framed the leaded windows; overstuffed couches and chairs filled the sitting room, and however much the crackling log-fire danced within the cavernous stone-hearth that inspired the name of the manor house, the flat, dark stonework seemed to reflect the gloom of the entire chamber—of the entire place, when you come right down to it.

"Onward we marched—Owen, his mother, and I—past a curving staircase carpeted in navy blue and into a well-stocked dining room barely illuminated by a few sconces hanging above the dark-wood sideboards and heavy serving tables. Each place-setting upon the dinner table itself looked fit for a king—or, I guess, for a queen, if one considered Mrs. Cobb as such. At least, the sparkling crystal, the shiny silver service, and the fine white china offered a degree of contrast to the darkness of the surroundings.

"There were seven chairs at the table. I figured that the one at the head was for the hostess, and an additional two were for her son and daughter-in-law. But besides another chair for me, I didn't know whom the other three places were for.

"At that moment, Owen entered the dining room with his wife.

"'Ham,' Lucille exclaimed, her blonde hair bouncing as she rushed towards me, "it's so wonderful to see you over here.'"

Garland paused, seemingly to savour the memory. "Gentlemen, I cannot lie to you. Her American twang was music to my ears, and I won't deny that I appreciated having an energetic young woman throw her arms around me. Still, out of the corner of my eye I could detect the critical stare of Mrs. Cobb.

"Two others then came into the room. The first, a lithe young woman dressed in a tightly fitting frock of purple velveteen. With long, dark tresses and narrow eyes, she looked like a cat lying in wait. As attractive as she was, I knew to keep my distance. The other figure, a heavy, curly-haired young man, sporting a rust-coloured tweed jacket that barely covered his stomach, seemed unable to take his protruding eyes off Lucille. I sensed danger there as well.

"'My brother and sister,' Owen announced, 'Cedric and Charlotte Cobb.'

"Charlotte glanced my way with an alluring smile while Cedric was occupied positioning himself next to Lucille. Charlotte, I was soon to learn, had a career in dance cut short by illness. Cedric, a student for a brief time at the New College, Oxford, had been summarily removed from the world of academia for excessive drinking and a consequent cheating scandal. In baseball lingo, it must have felt like being yanked from the box in the middle of a big inning."

As unfamiliar as I was with Garland's Americanism, I certainly comprehended his meaning. Cedric Cobb was at low water. One assumed Holmes understood as well.

"Last to enter the dining room," Garland went on, "was an older woman of Mrs. Cobb's generation, her clear eyes twinkling, her expression most welcoming. The grey dress she wore matched her grey hair, which was tied at the back of her head with a red ribbon, the only bright colour about her person.

"'Aunt Lena,' Owen announced, 'my mother's younger sister.'

"With a smile in my direction, Aunt Lena—so she invited me to call her—took the corner-seat to Mrs. Cobb's left, a sign for the rest of us to find our own places. Owen sat opposite his aunt at Mrs. Cobb's right; Lucille sat next to him. Cedric claimed the seat by Lucille's side, and Charlotte settled in next to Lena. That left the space next to Charlotte for me."

Quite a group, I thought.

Sherlock Holmes put it more succinctly. "The *dramatis personae* of this mystery play, I presume. What happened next?"

"Nothing really," Garland replied. "Oh, you couldn't miss the obvious family tensions—Owen's distaste for the way Cedric was cosying up to Lucille; Aunt Lena's timid glances at her domineering sister; Charlotte's lack of interest in most everything said; and, lording her power over everyone, the imposing figure of Muriel Cobb. I don't believe I needed to come to England to experience such a family; I'm certain I could have found similar interactions among the elite in Chicago or Boston as well."

More class consciousness on Garland's part, I noted, but at least his criticism crossed the Atlantic in both directions.

"Nor did matters improve with the arrival of the main course," Garland continued. "Bookman is the greying butler and husband of the cook. When he brought in the tray with the roast beef, the meat was, as I feared, black around the edges.

"'Apologies from the kitchen,' Bookman said softly.

Mrs. Cobb took one look at the proffered meal and in lamenting its charred condition, actually blamed the guest. 'I trust, Mr. Garland, you will not consider my cook responsible for any shortcomings in tonight's meal. *She* is certainly not the one to hold accountable.'"

"Quite the lack of civility, Mr. Garland," I observed, shaking my head. "Please, don't base your judgment of English courtesy on the behaviour of a female martinet."

This time Sherlock Holmes pointed his pipe stem at me. "Do not forget, Watson, that Garland could not have been the only target of Mrs. Cobb's displeasure. After all, as he himself has told us, the woman in question, Muriel Cobb, was the putative victim of a murderer. Is that not the point of your narrative, Garland?"

"Indeed, Holmes, if one is to believe Owen's words about the death of his mother. But I for one need more evidence to reach such a conclusion. I am the son of a former soldier, and I've been taught that it is my duty to get to the bottom of things. My father would want it no other way. He is my captain, after all; I, a mere corporal in the rear ranks."

"Quite," my friend said, showing no inkling at all to delve into Garland's familial ties or the interpretation of them by the fellow himself. On the contrary, Holmes waved his long fingers in an incoming fashion. "Let us finally have the facts of this crime then, man," he pleaded, "so we may judge for ourselves the possibility that this murder—if, as you imply, there really was one—ever took place."

Garland rose to his feet. "I can do better than that. Indulge me for a moment longer." So saying, he retrieved the valise of *faux*-leather that he had placed by the door and returning to his seat, quickly opened it. He moved aside the red cricket ball about which he had spoken and withdrew from the small suitcase a handsome notebook bound in brown morocco-leather.

"My diary, gentlemen," said he, holding up the book. "Through the decades, I've recorded occasional accounts of my comings and goings, but on January first of last year I began writing on a daily basis, a habit I have maintained during this trip." [*]

---

[*] Garland continued his daily reports until his death in March of 1940. His diary's forty-three volumes are collected in the Huntington Library in San Marino, California.

44

Garland opened the notebook and riffled through any number of pages of foolscap, each filled on both sides with a spidery handwriting that from where I was sitting looked scarcely decipherable. After finding the section he sought, he produced a small, bone-handled clasp-knife from a pocket and began carefully separating one page at a time from the leather binding. He removed about twenty sheets, stacked them together, and presented the collection to Sherlock Holmes.

"If you read this," the American said, "I believe you will get a more detailed account of the events at Hearthstone Hall than anything I might be able to tell you."

"Surely, you'll want the pages returned," I said.

"No need," Garland answered with a wave of his hand. "Better that my writings help Holmes resolve the matter."*

---

* It should be noted that the absence of these diary pages would not be considered particularly unusual by Garland's biographers. In her memoir, *A Summer to Be*, daughter Isabel Garland Lord remembers that diary pages dealing with other events in the author's life "had been torn out and presumably destroyed." In addition, an accompanying footnote to Lord's memoir by Garland-scholar Kevin Newlin refers to "removed pages" and "redated" entries.

"When did you write it all?" I asked, admittedly shocked that a man of letters would relinquish his work so casually.

"I made the first Hearthstone entry Saturday night and added more late Sunday before I tried falling asleep. I began the rest early this morning and finished it on the train back here to London."

I moved my chair next to Holmes, who was already thumbing eagerly through the pages. When I was suitably positioned, Holmes turned back to Saturday's entry, and together the two of us silently decoded the crabbed handwriting before us. What follows is Hamlin Garland's account of the disquieting events he witnessed beginning but two nights before in Hearthstone Hall.

One need not possess the gift of foresight to intuit that in addition to the details about the manor house Garland presented to us in his diary, future events would inevitably lead us back not only to the disturbing relationships within the Cobb family but also to the fateful landscape already characterised as the Devil's Punch Bowl.

Chapter Four

Hamlin Garland's Diary

> The importance of Garland's diaries is not that they startle us with a portrait of a "new" Garland. Their interest lies in the range of his activities as an American man of letters and in the depth of his response to the conditions of his life.
> —Donald Piser
> "Introduction"
> *Hamlin Garland's Diaries*

Saturday Night
May 6, 1899
Hearthstone Hall

If one could overlook my tardiness this evening, which Mrs. Cobb seemed singularly unable to do, the dinner of (slightly-burnt) beefsteak proceeded uneventfully. Bookman, the butler, did the serving, his wife did the cooking, and he returned to remove the dishes from the table.

Not long thereafter, Mrs. Bookman led me to the grim-looking bed-chamber in which I now pen these lines. Replete with dark walls, heavy drapes, and black-walnut furniture—a small table by the door and the high bed with its burgundy-colored canopy in particular—a gloomier place I find difficult to imagine. The entire manor house exudes an oppressive quality, and my room appears no different. It is as if all the contents of the house had been put together in the previous century and, though Mrs. Cobb has quite a lot of money (if Owen is to be believed), not much of it has been spent on beautifying her home.

Late Sunday Afternoon
May 7, 1899
Hearthstone Hall

The day began innocently enough despite the dark clouds hovering above. Would that it ended in a similar fashion. Following a spartan breakfast of a rasher of bacon and a single egg (despite a chicken coop full of clucking hens), Lucille grabbed my arm and suggested we navigate a morning hike through the nearby hills.

"Have a coat, Miss," Mrs. Bookman said in a motherly fashion. "There's a storm on the way."

Lucille grabbed a blue scarf and the nearest coat from a line of them hanging on hooks in the entry hall. "We all share coats around here," she explained, shoving the scarf into a pocket. "It's simpler."

Her selection turned out to be a roomy, dark-blue pea jacket, and when she slipped into it, the coarse-wool coat and her decidedly-feminine tweed skirt and lavender scent resulted in an obvious incongruity.

Nonetheless, Mrs. Bookman nodded approvingly, and when I donned my sombrero and perched the brim at just the right jaunty angle, she nodded again.

Despite the gloomy day—or, perhaps, because of it—as Lucille and I stepped outside, I joked, "No jobs for you this morning? Mrs. Cobb couldn't find some extra work for you to do?"

"Why, yes, actually," Lucille said with only the hint of a smile, "she did give me a job. Since Owen is checking on the animals with Fairley, she assigned me the laborious task of looking after you. Far be it from my mother-in-law to assume so tiring a role." More seriously, she added, "Mother Cobb's all too quick to give Charlotte and me any jobs that come along—most of them, the jobs she pays the Bookmans to do."

"Oh, I can't believe things are as bad as that," I said.

By way of explanation, Lucille motioned me to follow her to the back of the house. We passed a small cottage where she told me the Bookmans lived, *and she pointed out the barn and stables beyond it. A moment later, we entered a courtyard laid with uneven slabs of rust-colored flagstone. At its center stood a large, twisted oak tree in whose shadow, as Lucille pointed out, lay a large, wooden crate.*

"Meet Oliver," she said. A chorus of barks greeted her as she freed from its tether within the crate a small, brindled terrier that had been reclining, head down, upon a thick, gray blanket. On seeing Lucille, the little dog leaped up in excitement.

"He seems happy enough," I said, bending low to scratch behind his ears when he came by to sniff at me.

"He is—now that I've come to rescue him from his prison out here. Owen and I brought him with us all the way from Chicago, but Mother Cobb won't let him stay in the house. 'He'll just be under foot,' she says. So he has to remain outside in the cold and face the elements."

Beneath the ever-darkening sky, Lucille let the dog run off ahead, and the two of us followed him along a slowly-rising footpath. The trail ran parallel to a long, wood-rail fence off to our left. It couldn't have been more than thirty yards from the house, and it was interrupted at its center by a wooden stile.

"Why is there a fence over there?" I asked, pointing at the railing.

"To keep people away from the fifty-foot cliff on the other side. The locals call the place Demon's

Drop, and the fencing is to prevent anyone from straying too close to the edge. Thick brush covers much of the area, so it would be all too easy to make a false step and tumble over. If you need to, you can get past the fence by way of the stile, but there are less-dangerous views of the Punch Bowl to be had than that one. I'll show you."

With Oliver in the lead, we marched on.

"Mrs. Bookman was right about the rain," I said pointing to the thick, black clouds. "It looks like a storm is fast approaching."

Lucille glanced up, but she was clearly concerned with weightier matters than the weather. "I was surprised when I heard you were coming to England, Ham," she said as we continued along a maze of weed-filled paths. In a few of the steepest inclines, stone steps had been installed to help hikers negotiate the climbs. "I guess I was really more surprised to learn that you were able to tear yourself away from Zulime. I thought you were in intense pursuit of her."

A jolt of annoyance ran through me. I had forsaken much more than Zulime when I left Chicago. Truth be told, I guess I blamed Zulime for the unfinished stories, plays, and novels I had also left behind.

"Not that it's any of your business, Lucille," I said coldly, "but her brother Lorado informed me when I got back to Chicago in March that 'Sister

Zuhl' was engaged to someone else. So much for my secret dreams!"

Lucille shook her head.

"Once I learned that news" I told Lucille, "I became disheartened. I really didn't want to stay in Chicago any longer. I'd sought companionship from Zulime. Lorado's words hurt me; they made me angry. I needed to get out of town."

"Oh, Ham," was all Lucille could say.

"You know, I've done a lot of traveling in the last few years. I've been to the 'High Country' out west, and I've just come back from a five-month trip to the gold fields of the Yukon Valley. But this time, I was looking to cross the sea. England has always interested me, and friends like Owen have offered me invitations, so here I am."

Lucille punched me lightly on the shoulder. "Oh, Ham," she said again, only this time with a sympathetic smile, "your reasoning makes sense, but you can't give up on Zuhl so easily. You have to understand. Ever since Turbie[*] married one of Lorado's pals, he's worried about losing other friends to his sisters—in this case, you to Zulime. That's why he told you she was engaged to someone else—to put you off the hunt."

---

[*] Zulime's father, Don Carlos Taft, a professor of geology, was enchanted by classical names. He called his son Lorado Zadok and his three daughters, Zulime Maune, Florisel Adino, and Turbulance Doctoria.

"A moment," I said, having a hard time comprehending. "Am I to understand that Zulime let him get away with such subterfuge?"

"As of now," Lucille laughed, "he hasn't gotten away with anything. Whether he succeeds or not, I guess is really up to you."

"Maledictions on Lorado!" I exclaimed. I could still recall from just weeks before the scene in which the black-bearded Lorado had broken the news to me—how the slender sculptor stood there in his frock coat, his expressive eyes full of what I now know to be false sympathy, and warned me away from his sister. Although I remember thinking he looked embarrassed when he delivered the fateful words, it's still hard to believe that in spite of all the dignity I attributed to him, he was lying.

"I have to write to Zulime," I told Lucille. "I have to tell her I'm coming back to Chicago. I intend to marry the girl. My aging mother continues to demand a daughter."

Lucille laughed again and put a hand on my arm. "Don't get so excited, Ham. Knowing how the mail runs, you'll probably get to Chicago before a letter from here does. Calm down. Enjoy your stay. Come on. I'll show you some English history."

I still felt nettled, but less so. With Oliver scampering ahead, I let Lucille guide me over a few small hillocks, through countless shadows, and up a slope towards the rim of the Punch Bowl.

"Despite its bloody history," she said when we reached the top, "it's really quite lovely up here." And she stretched her arm over the vista that spread out before us.

Oh, the beauty of the place! I'd seen the Punch Bowl on my ride to Hearthstone the day before, but now that I had the chance to actually contemplate the landscape and inhale its sweet, honied fragrance, I could appreciate the natural glory that exists alongside the gloom.

Below me lay large swaths of pink bilberries, white heather, and yellow gorse, the colorful patchwork interrupted here and there by any number of curious rock-formations. Meandering ribbons of water and the occasional turbid pool at the very bottom of the basin managed to reflect the few rays of light that penetrated the darkness.

"It's quite lovely," I told Lucille. "It reminds me of where I grew up in Wisconsin. Only there we had snakes."

"Oh, then you should feel right at home. There are adders here, 'vipers' some call them. They leave us alone if we let them be—although little Oliver doesn't know that. I worry about him."

Serpents, I thought, adding to the grimness.

As if to underscore such concerns, Lucille led me across a gorse-covered hillock where to my surprise she pointed to what looked like a gravestone planted right there in the middle of nowhere.

"Read that," she instructed. *"It helps explain the gloom."*

I copied it down word-for-word; here's what I read:

ERECTED
In detestation of a barbarous Murder
Committed here on an unknown Sailor
On Sep, 24th 1786
By Edwd. Lonegon, Mich. Casey & Ja^s. Marshall
Who were all taken the same day
And hung in Chains near this place
Whoso sheddeth Man's Blood by Man shall his
Blood be shed. Gen Chap 9 Ver 6

If all that wasn't sufficiently morbid, the text on the back of the stone included the following:

Cursed be the Man who injureth
or removeth this Stone[*]

"The three villains—killers, actually," Lucille explained, *"were caught and executed. Then their bodies were preserved in tar and hung in chains from a gibbet as a warning to others. Cedric said the bodies were up for years. I'll show you the spot."*

---

[*] The Sailor's Stone exists to this day near the site of the sailor's murder. The actual gravestone stands in the Thursley churchyard, Surrey, where the sailor is buried.

I followed her along a narrow footpath to the top of a hillock where a tall Celtic cross made of granite stood silhouetted against the leaden sky.

"The locals put the cross here to drive away the evil spirits," Lucille said. "It's the site of the old gibbet. That's why they call this place Gibbet Hill."

What a frightful history, I thought, even with the beautiful landscape.

"I first came here a few weeks ago," Lucille said. "Cedric thought it was a good time for me to learn about the neighborhood, especially since Owen and the others were occupied playing bridge."

She gave a little shudder, and I felt that something uncomfortable was coming. I wasn't wrong.

"Silly me," she said. "I was foolish enough to believe that he wanted to talk about the history of the area. But then he tried kissing me—me, his brother's wife! I pushed him away—"

"No small task, a man his size," *I interrupted with not a little disgust. As uncomfortable as I was to hear more about the encounter, I was nonetheless pleased with Lucille's response. I know that if I am ever fortunate enough to have a daughter, I'll do what I can to keep her out of such situations. But if I fail, I hope she'll have the fortitude of Lucille Cobb.*

"Did you tell Owen?" *I asked.*

"No. I just demanded that Cedric take me back to Hearthstone."

"Tell me he did."

"Yes, he did, but not before he confessed that he loved me. Mother Cobb was standing at the door when we came in, and she gave me one of those critical stares she's so good at. Cedric went on his way, but Mother Cobb pulled me aside."

I couldn't imagine reporting to a mother such inappropriate action by her son.

"I must admit," said Lucille, "that I was reluctant to tell her what Cedric was up to, but before I could utter a word, she raised an eyebrow and gave me her advice. 'You know, Lucille," she said, "men are irrational beings. It is up to us women to control them. We have the power, and whatever men attempt to do to us, we possess the wiles to turn them away. Don't expect me to feel sorry for you. On the contrary, I compliment your strength. Be sure you use it wisely."

Lucille smiled in the gloom. "Despite that evil business with Cedric, I still like to come out here and look at the hollow. It's quite peaceful, you know."

Oliver, the little terrier, went bounding off to examine the countryside, and a few caw-cawing crows circled beneath the thick black clouds that were scudding in our direction.

As morning turned to afternoon, we began walking again, and when I saw Lucille quickly wipe away tears, I looked at her more closely. Small lines of worry showed around her eyes and her lips.

"What's wrong?" I asked.

She stopped and grabbed my arm. "Oh, Ham," she cried, "I don't know how much longer I can tolerate all this."

At first, I laughed. "I grant you your husband's family is strange. but you've got Owen to protect you. I daresay that if you tell him about it, he won't put up with the kind of nonsense you've described with Cedric."

Lucille shook her head. "You don't understand, Ham. It's not Cedric who bothers me; I can deal with him. It's Mother Cobb."

"Surely, you're not letting that old lady bother you. I can see that she's unduly strict and that your dog has to live outside, but—"

"She has me working all day long, Ham. If I'm not cleaning the house or tending the flowers, I'm helping Mrs. Bookman with the wash. It's not like my mother-in-law isn't able to pay for more help. She's rich! She just doesn't want to spend. Her motto is, 'Why waste money on servants when family can do just as well?' She has Owen working all the time too. That's why he and not some hired manager is out with Fairley right now looking in on the chickens. She wants someone like Owen whom she knows she can trust making certain that jobs are being properly done."

I shook my head. "You forget, Lucille, that I grew up on a farm. Your mother-in-law has a point about keeping an eye on the work of others."

Lucille dropped my arm. "You too, Ham? Owen takes her side on everything. Maybe it's the way you men deal with intimidating women. If you want to know the truth, the longer Owen works here, the more like her I think he's becoming."

"What else?" I dared to ask.

"Okay," she said. "Two weeks ago, Charlotte and I went into Haslemere with Bookman. He drove the wagon, and the two of us sat in the back so we could talk. Charlotte's a dancer, you know, but about a year ago she had to stop when she developed pneumonia. Breathing was difficult—obviously, a real problem for a dancer—and her mother invited her home to recuperate."

"Quite reasonable," I said.

"Yes," Lucille agreed, "that's what I thought at first." She crossed her arms in front of her chest to tell me the next part: "Except during that time, even though Charlotte had recuperated, her partner, Claude, rehearsed a new dancer, so Charlotte, in order to get back on the stage with him, needed fresh costumes and train-tickets to wherever Claude was performing. Somewhere in the north, I believe. Charlotte asked her mother for 125 pounds, and her mother said no. It's not that Mother Cobb can't afford it. It's that she wants to control her children."

I shook my head again.

The footpath took a turn downhill, and Hearthstone Hall came back into view, its gray walls blending with the dark clouds above. We were walking faster now, and Lucille quickened her narrative to be sure she finished enumerating her complaints before we reached the house.

"On another occasion" she told me, "I wrote a letter to Zuhl and discovered that I didn't have any stamps or even the cash to buy them. I couldn't ask Owen because he was off in the hog-pens that afternoon, so I asked my mother-in-law to loan me a bank note. Obviously, I hadn't learned the lesson, for I received the same answer that Charlotte had gotten. In a word, 'No.' I was so angry that I packed my bags to leave right then."

"But you're still here," I pointed out.

Lucille smiled. "Only after I threatened to return to Chicago did Mother Cobb agree that she had overreacted."

"But she did admit her mistake, Lucille. Surely, you can see that."

Lucille frowned. "I don't trust her, Ham. Don't you understand? It's like we're prisoners here. The reason I was so excited to see you last night is that I know you'll be returning to the States soon, and I want to leave this place when you do. I want to go back to Chicago where I don't have these terrible feelings."

"*And leave Owen? Go with* me *and leave your husband? What does Owen have to say about how his mother treats you?*"

"*I don't know what he thinks. For some reason, I promised Mother Cobb that I wouldn't say anything to Owen about our disagreement over the stamps. Owen keeps telling me that I'm just homesick, that soon I'll feel better about living here, that all I have to do is learn to understand his mother the way he does.*"

"*That sounds like good, practical advice.*"

"*Then he told me how much he loves me and how he would be lost without me. But when I said that he and I should go back to Chicago together, he said no. He said his mother's now too dependent upon him. Oh, how I wish we could be rid of the woman.*"

Lucille ended her story just as we passed the fence by Demon's Drop. At the same time, a light rain began to fall, and she withdrew the scarf from her pocket and covered her blond hair. Clapping her hands to bring Oliver back to us, she announced with a note of finality, "Let's go home."

I couldn't tell if she was talking to me or to the dog, and I didn't know if she was referring to Hearthstone or Chicago. What I did know was that in spite of my hat, water had begun seeping down the back of my neck and into my shirt. We had spent most all of the day in conversation, and it was time to get back to the house.

Upon our return, Lucille led a reluctant Oliver into his crate and reattached the leash. As the two of us entered through the front door, she said, "We should have just enough time to change for dinner."

"Change?"

"Oh," Lucille blushed, "didn't I tell you? Mother Cobb said tonight's affair will be formal."

To all the family business Lucille had given me to ponder, I now had to add donning my swallow-tail and its accoutrements. Thank goodness for Zangwill's help in London! What's more, considering my poor timing the night before, at all cost I had to avoid being late.

Lost in thought, I barely missed running into Charlotte at the front door. As I was closing it, she rushed by Lucille and slipped past me. I held the door open for her as once outside, she stared up at the sky and then did a quick about-face and hurried back in.

"Thin rain, dark clouds, and a flicker of lightning over the rim of the Punch Bowl," she reported. "Conclusion? A great thunderstorm tonight."

Aunt Lena, who was just coming down the stairs, heard Charlotte's prediction. "I hope not,"

Aunt Lena said. "You know how terrifying I find thunder and lightning."

Charlotte rolled her eyes at Lucille and me. "Ever since she was a child, Aunt Lena's been deathly afraid of thunderstorms. At least, that's what she's told us. When she was little, she'd hide under her bed or in any available cabinet."

At that moment, Mrs. Cobb appeared at the top of the staircase, so in a quieter voice, Charlotte whispered, "I'm sure it didn't help that Aunt Lena's older sister—our mother—made fun of her."

"Don't tell me you're still talking about your fear of lightning, Lena," Mrs. Cobb said as she descended the stairs. "As I've instructed you thousands of times, you've got to get over such nonsense."

"Sorry, Muriel," Lena said. "I keep trying."

"Notice," Lucille whispered in my ear, "how many times people say 'sorry' to my mother-in-law."

I knew exactly what she meant. In point of fact, "sorry" was my very first word to the woman.

Late Sunday Night
May 7, 1899
Hearthstone Hall

I had no idea how vicious the night would become.

At first, I thought it would just be ridiculous! For someone like me who had grown up in austerity, a formal dinner seemed pointless—especially after learning so many disturbing facts about the people who were to sit at the table.

Still, I extracted from my valise the neatly folded, swallow-tail coat and along with my black trousers, high collar, and white tie, I do believe I presented an acceptable image as I entered the dining room right on time.

With rain now enveloping the house, the candlelight from the sconces around us seemed all the more somber. In contrast to the festive gatherings at Blen Cathra and Undershaw, the mood at Hearthstone matched the stiff formality of the setting. Cedric and Owen, the other males in the group, wore black, but to their credit the women brought in some color.

Mrs. Cobb was attired in a white, beaded dress with a modest neckline just low enough to show off the golden necklace and sparkling diamonds that hung around her throat. Gracing a finger was an elaborate gold ring highlighted by a pair of entwined serpents, their elaborate heads and forked tongues separated by an oval-shaped, blood-red ruby.

Her sister Lena was dressed in a full-skirted, light-blue gown; daughter Charlotte, in a narrow-skirted blue dress cut low enough to reveal more of her body than seemed appropriate; and Lucille, in a yellow gown with white piping. Bookman the butler wore a formal outfit for the occasion while his wife, who briefly emerged from the kitchen, covered her green dress with a white apron.

We began with Mrs. Bookman's tomato bisque. As we sipped, I attempted to engage the group with a report of Lucille's and my day-long walk to the Devil's Punch Bowl. I fear, however, that I dwelled too long on how the place reminded me of my childhood home in Wisconsin, for when Bookman reappeared to remove the soup dishes, it seemed a relief to my companions that his actions cut short my account.

Minutes later, the butler returned with the main course. Had a trumpet fanfare announced his arrival, it could not have been more dramatic. In his formal uniform, Bookman marched slowly into the room bearing in his outstretched arms a large silver-domed salver that reflected the flames from the flickering candles. Slowly, he placed the offering on the table in front of Mrs. Cobb.

With great deference, the butler raised the shiny dome to reveal a magnificent roast suckling pig, complete with the proverbial red apple in its mouth. I could recall celebrating many the happy occasion in my own youth with just such a feast. Yet no sooner did Bookman, dome in hand, step back, than I observed Lucille, perhaps more sensitive than usual, blanch at the sight of the caramel-colored pig carcass.

Once Bookman had returned to the kitchen, Mrs. Cobb rose and carefully selected from in front of her plate a pair of essential instruments—a large, two-pronged silver fork and a shiny, ivory-handled carving knife. Delicately inserting the fork near the darkened joint of the pig's foreleg, she brought the gleaming knife-blade down slowly and began the initial cut.

Suddenly, Lucille shrieked, and we all turned to look at the poor girl as before our eyes she swooned and slumped towards Owen seated next to her.

Nor did the drama end there, for startled by Lucille's cry, Mrs. Cobb involuntarily jerked the knife, gashing her wrist in the process, spilling bright red blood over the sleeve of her white dress.

Aunt Lena burst into tears, and while Charlotte didn't move, Cedric sprang awkwardly to his feet, almost knocking over his chair. For his part, Owen sat Lucille upright and rubbed her wrists. It took but a moment for her to revive, and Owen pressed a glass of water to her lips.

She managed a sip or two, coughed a few times, and finally presented a weak smile. "I-I'm fine," she murmured, her face pale. "You can sit down, Cedric. It's just that the pig looked—it looked—oh, it looked like a human child—a baby—

and when the knife pierced the skin—well, I—I couldn't watch."

At the sound of all the chaos, Bookman had rushed back into the room and assuming an authoritative role, grabbed Mrs. Cobb's white napkin and wrapped it around her wounded wrist.

"You need not worry about me," Mrs. Cobb said even as the butler tightened the knot.

Once Bookman saw that the cloth was secure, he carried the dinner back to the kitchen where, out of Lucille's sight, the pig was carved and soon brought back to the table. Even more somber than before, we resumed eating with not even a snide remark available to fill the air. Only the drumbeat of the rain against the windows interrupted the silence.

Which is not to say that I wasn't replaying the dramatic scene in my mind. I assume that we all were, except for Mrs. Cobb. As befits the proud leader of a clan, she proceeded through her dinner as if nothing extraordinary—the fainting drama and a knife slicing into her wrist!—had ever occurred.

Mrs. Bookman's rice pudding concluded the meal, and Cedric suggested that Owen and I remain at the table for cigars. No one had been in a conversive mood following Lucille's outburst, however, and I, having listened to Lucille's complaints for most of the afternoon, had little interest in spending additional time with her brother or husband.

We were about to adjourn to the warmth of the living-room fire when Mrs. Cobb announced that Lucille should get some rest.

"You've had quite enough excitement for one evening," Mrs. Cobb said to her. "Come upstairs, and I shall give you the same sedative I take myself whenever I have trouble falling asleep."

"Really, I feel all right," Lucille protested, but Mrs. Cobb raised her hand to silence her daughter-in-law. "Don't dawdle," she advised over her shoulder as she retreated up the stairs.

"Do what Mother says," Owen cautioned, "and everything will be fine."

Lucille remained in her seat, but I couldn't help thinking that, like the ambiguities expressed earlier by his wife, Owen, in referring to his mother's immediate instructions, might well have been talking about how to live life in general.

Strangely, it took but a few moments after we had settled ourselves in the living room for Mrs. Cobb to reappear. And when she did, she was in a huff. "Charlotte! Charlotte!" she shouted as she came marching down the stairs.

Charlotte jerked her head in her mother's direction, but said nothing.

"You were straightening up my room earlier," her mother charged. "What did you do to my medicine?"

Charlotte said nothing.

Cedric merely smirked.

"Charlotte?" Aunt Lena whispered.

"Charlotte!" her mother barked.

The girl's mouth gaped wide. "What?" she murmured at last. "Your medicine? What did I do to your medicine? Why, nothing. I did nothing to your medicine. What do you mean?"

Mrs. Cobb held up a small, glass bottle so all of us could see it. The glass itself was clear, but the liquid inside appeared a murky green. "You must have done something to it."

"I did nothing to your precious medicine."

Mrs. Cobb arched both eyebrows. "This is my sleeping bromide. It is supposed to be colorless, but as you can see, it is now green. Green!" she repeated loudly, raising the bottle even higher. "Green—the color of arsenic."

"Mother," Owen said, "Just because it's green doesn't—"

"Someone tried to kill me, I say," Mrs. Cobb interrupted and turned back to her daughter. "Charlotte, I can only wonder if you had something to do with it."

The poor girl was speechless. Indeed, no one had anything to say. The pulsating rain added to the melodrama.

Mrs. Cobb eyed each one of us individually. Then quite dramatically, she turned to the dancing flames in the middle of the hearthstone fireplace and hurled the tainted bottle against its stone rear-wall. The glass shattered into a thousand pieces, and as the bilious green liquid pooled over the floor at the back of the hearth, a pungent, chemical smell filled the air.

"Be advised, all of you," Mrs. Cobb proclaimed angrily. "I have my own method for fighting back." With those words she turned and mounted the stairs, accompanied—however coincidentally—by ominous peals of distant thunder.

Moments later, Charlotte too marched up the stairs, and we all heard her door slam shut.

"I've had enough as well," said Cedric. "I'm going out. The smell in here is terrible."

"It's pouring rain," said Owen.

"I'm only going to Bookman's. Fairley's brought a new supply of whisky. What better way to brave a storm?" He left through the front door, returning only for a moment to collect an umbrella.

Seated across from me, Aunt Lena closed her eyes and crossed her arms. Presumably, she hoped to protect herself from whatever the rumbling in the *heavens foretold. Flashes of lightning lit up the windows. Owen remained silent.*

It took but a few minutes for Mrs. Cobb to appear yet again. From the living room, you could see her on the landing. She wore a blue robe over a cream-colored nightgown, the gown's high lace collar covering her neck, its lace cuffs at her wrists extending outward from beneath the robe's sleeves. No expert on women's sleep ware, I assumed she intended the cuff to conceal her ugly bout with the carving knife.

The family matriarch leaned over the wooden rail and calmly addressed her older son "Owen, I have some business matters I'd like to discuss with you. Please come up here."

You couldn't miss the change in her voice. Gone was the angry tone she had employed a few minutes earlier.

For some reason, Owen glared silently at Lucille and me as he left the living room, climbed the stairs, and joined his mother as she retreated into her bedroom.

Moments later, Aunt Lena rose and walked slowly up the stairs as well.

* * *

Lucille and I were alone now. Nonetheless, her words came to me in whispers. "He's becoming more like her every day. He likes the way she runs things. He likes the farm-work she gives him. He likes handing out orders to the Bookmans and to Fairley. And to the rest of us. Just like her, he seeks to control everyone. And even worse, poet that he is—or was—he hasn't written anything since he's been here, not even an obscene limerick."

"Are you sure you're being fair, Lucille?" I asked. "Overseeing Hearthstone is rather new for him, you know."

She just shook her head. "Would you believe it, Ham? When you and I came back from our walk this afternoon, he complained that I was spending too much time with you. I believe he sounded jealous."

"You're not serious?" I said, beginning to understand the hostile look Owen had just cast at the two of us.

"He's not the man I married, Ham. I can't stay with him any longer. I have to go back to Chicago."

Despite what I was hearing, Owen was my friend. I wanted no part of helping his wife leave their marriage. "We'll talk about this tomorrow. You've had quite the night. Let's go upstairs."

We reached the landing just in time to hear Owen offering a tender good night to his mother at her door. When he turned and saw Lucille and me, a frown washed over his face, but as he was about to speak, Charlotte's door opened, and the three of us watched Mrs. Bookman scurry out of Charlotte's room, shut the door, and rush down the servants' back stairway. We all exchanged questioning glances, and Lucille and I followed Owen as he marched towards his sister's room.

"Charlotte," he cried out as he knocked on the door, "is everything all right?"

"Go away," came the response.

"Charlotte," he said, placing his hand on the doorknob, "I'm coming in." He opened the door a crack, but from inside Charlotte slammed it shut. "Go away!" she shouted again.

Owen backed up and proceeded to focus his attention on Lucille and me. He took a few steps towards us, put his arm around Lucille's waist, and without saying a word steered her down the hallway and into their bedroom. He shut the door with a sense of finality.

I trailed after them, passing their door and moving on to the end of the corridor and my own room. Though the walls are thick in an old manor-house like Hearthstone, before I left the corridor, I could hear Owen's raised voice invoking my name, and I paused to listen.

"Don't think I'm blind to what's going on between you and Garland," Owen was shouting. "I saw the two of you. I may have invited him here, but I know that you spent the day with him and that on the morrow you're planning to run off together to the States. I won't have it, Lucille! I'm your husband, and I'm telling you to stay."

I had no idea how Owen had learned of Lucille's intentions. For all I knew, she had told him herself. In any case, I heard nothing else for a minute or two. Maybe there were a few sobs, but I couldn't be sure. Finally, Lucille said, "You're right, Owen. You are my husband, and I'm bound to stay. But tonight I don't want to look at you."

A moment later their door opened and out stepped Owen. He saw me in the hall, but said nothing and shuffled his way down the stairs.

Once he was out of sight, I entered my own room, lit a candle, and carefully put away my formal togs. It was time to write.

* * *

Oppression blankets the house. I can only wonder how many others feel it. Certainly, the dog, Oliver, has expressed his dismay. How else to interpret the little terrier's tremulous wailing in the rain? One has to sympathize with his complaints that came to an end with a single brief but defiant yelp. Perhaps, he sensed that the storm was going to end, or maybe he understood that even worse was on the way.

It feels close within my bedchamber, and despite the downpour, I have opened a window for fresh air. Ever louder grows the thrum of the falling drops beyond the window. The more intense it grows, the more I fear that in the hours ahead, sleep will remain beyond my reach.

Early Monday Morning
May 8, 1899
Hearthstone Hall

The roar ripped through the night like an explosion. A harbinger of worse to come, it shook the house and jolted me out of the fitful sleep in which I somehow found myself. My pocket-watch next to the bed showed just past one o'clock, and because of the window I'd left open, the rain came splashing through and the hair-raising crash from outside sounded all the louder. I sat bolt upright and, witnessing a strange light flaring in the untamed gardens below my room, I got to my feet and staggered towards the window.

Oh, the brightness of it all! Fire lit up the courtyard. In the center, the grotesque limbs of the oak tree seeming to writhe in the flames. There was no mystery as to the cause, no question of what had happened. The noble oak had been cleft in two and set afire by a well-directed bolt of lightning.*

Poor Oliver. The small dog had a front-row seat to the fireworks, and his silence suggested how frightened he was.

But I had no time for contemplating the lightning's effect on the dog or on anyone else. More important was how the house was holding up. Quickly, I donned my shirt and trousers and headed downstairs.

I assumed that like myself everyone else had been awakened by the deafening blast and would be assembling in the living room. I'd gotten it mainly right. Owen was present, but then he had already been sleeping downstairs. Cedric, no doubt having just returned from his drinking spree in Bookman's cottage, was doing his best to light the candles despite his trembling hands. Minutes later, their hair askew and clutching their robes about them, Charlotte and Lucille joined the group.

Appropriately enough, it was Owen who took charge. "We must check that the house has not been

---

* Coincidentally, Garland's account of the tree struck by lightning would be echoed years later in *The Man from Morocco* (1920) by Edgar Wallace, the writer whose works helped convince Garland to accept the mystery genre as legitimate literature. More predictably, a similar scene appears in *Abandon Hope* (1941) by Garland's daughter, Isabel Lord, her fictional account of the same events that appear in *The Hearthstone Manuscript*.

hit and that nothing else is burning," he said. Following that proclamation, he handed Cedric and me random coats from the hooks near the front door and slipped into one himself. I had the presence of mind to grab my hat, and the three of us marched out into the wet night to inspect the grounds.

Lightning continued to flicker in the distance, and thunder still shook the air, but fortunately it took only a few minutes to survey the building and its surroundings to ascertain that all was in order. Oh, we received a good drenching, but having discovered nothing else on fire and no parts of the structure assaulted, we were only too happy to return to the dry indoors and rid ourselves of our wet coats.

Once safely inside, we found that Charity Bookman, still in her dress and apron, had joined Lucille and Charlotte in the living room. She had also begun a fire in the hearth.

"Everything's fine," Owen told the women.

"Where's Bookman?" Cedric demanded of the butler's wife. "Why wasn't he out there helping us?"

"He's asleep in bed," Mrs. Bookman said as she nursed the flames.

"I was just with him," said Cedric. "If I can stand the rain, so can he."

"If you really were just at our cottage, Mr. Cedric," Mrs. Bookman charged, "then you know *how much he had to drink. When he's like that, I tell you, nothing wakes him up."*

"For that matter," Owen said, "where's Fairley?"

"More to the point," Charlotte demanded of Owen, "where is Mother?"

"And Aunt Lena," added Cedric. "She hasn't come down either."

"Aunt Lena's probably hiding under her bed," Owen offered. "We all know how lightning terrifies her. I can't imagine where Mother went off to. I'll go up and check on both of them." With those words, he bounded up the stairs.

Concern for the older women ended any talk of Fairley, and all we heard for the next few minutes was the drumroll of raindrops cascading against the window panes. After what seemed like a quarter of an hour but may have been much less, Owen appeared on the staircase. He who had so recently hurried up the stairs was now descending in a slow, trancelike walk. With his clear eyes open wide, he stared at all of us and announced quite simply, "Mother is dead."

* * *

Doubt and astonishment struggled in the faces around me.

"I checked her pulse," Owen said. "She's gone."

Slowly, people rose, and we all followed Owen back up the stairs to his mother's bedroom. The gas lamp by the side of the bed was still alight. The window was open a bit, and drips of water beaded on the carpet below it.

Lying beneath the white bedclothes with only her head and arms visible, Muriel Laughton Cobb looked as if she were sleeping. The white lace of her nightgown concealed her neck, and except for a wisp of the cloth napkin that Bookman had used to wrap the cut on her left wrist, the cream-colored sleeves and lace cuffs fully covered her arms. In repose, with her features relaxed and her eyes closed, she appeared less a tyrant than a tired old woman.

Charlotte leaned over her mother and gently kissed her forehead. At the other side of the bed, Cedric kissed the back of the dead woman's hand. Lucille put her arm around Owen's waist, and I stood respectfully in the background.

We remained standing quietly for a few minutes. Less emotionally involved than the others, I found myself examining various details in the room—from the side-wall, where hung a broad-brush painting of irises, to the various pieces of furniture like the large armoire beyond the foot of the bed; the dresser with its collection of scent bottles; the small table at bedside upon which stood a glass, *a water-pitcher, a bottle of gray pills, and a novel by one of the Brontës.*

It took a moment or two before I discerned a small scratch in the wood of the compact writing desk. It appeared on the facing of the bottom drawer just to the left of the slightly-distorted aperture, which was itself indicative of the jimmied lock at its center. My compliments to whoever had broken the tiny mechanism; it had been a neat job.

Hoping to avoid a commotion, I waited for the mourners to depart before I indicated the problem to Owen, and immediately he removed the drawer in question, opened the desktop, and shook the drawer over it. Nothing fell out. He muttered some oath, then closed the desk, and slid the drawer back into its slot.

"Time to go," he said and proceeded to close the window and extinguish the lamp.

Once we had left the room, Owen locked the door and, putting the key in his waistcoat pocket, led the way down the stairs. By the time we reached the living room, everyone else had already congregated there, everyone but the dead woman's sister.

"Aunt Lena is still missing," Charlotte said.

"Cedric, you look down here for her," Owen told his brother. "I'll go back upstairs."

"I already went to her room," said Charlotte, "and I didn't see her there."

"You probably didn't look in the right place," said Owen.

Ten minutes later, Owen came down the stairs again, this time leading his Aunt Lena who blinked timidly in his wake. Her hair looked plastered in place, and her lips trembled.

Owen delivered her to the open arms of Charlotte who settled in with her aunt on the couch.

A moment later, Cedric re-joined the group. "I see you've found her," he said to his brother.

"She was in her armoire," Owen explained, "hiding from the lightning. I've told her about the death of her sister—our mother."

Suddenly, Lucille exclaimed, "Owen, we've forgotten about Oliver."

"I'll get him," he said.

Owen returned a few minutes later. In his arms lay the whimpering Oliver, a streak of blood along his back.

Lucille bolted from her chair as soon as Owen entered and ran to comfort the dog. "What happened to him?"

"I don't know," Owen said.

Having learned a thing or two about animals from my experiences on my father's farms, I got up and approached the poor creature. Carefully examining a welt on the dog's back, I said, "It looks like something hit him."

"Or someone," added Cedric.

I remembered the yelp I'd heard earlier and the quiet that followed.

"Who would do such a thing?" Lucille demanded.

"Maybe a branch fell on him," I suggested.

Charlotte ignored me. "None of us could have done it," she observed. "We've all been in the house."

Cedric surveyed the group. "Not all of us are here," he said. "Where's Fairley? And Bookman's still missing."

As soon as he said the words, we all looked at the butler's wife.

"Again?" she complained. "Don't be charging Norton with anything," she said defiantly. "Have you all forgotten how he helped Mrs. Cobb when she cut her wrist? Right now, he's back in the cottage sleeping—like I told you. Never got out of bed, did he?"

"Oh, really, Mrs. Bookman," replied Cedric sarcastically. "As far as I can tell, you haven't been out in the rain. If you'd come from the cottage, your hair and your dress would be wet. But they don't appear to be."

"Slept on the cot in the kitchen, I did," Mrs. Bookman confessed. "You blokes doing all that drinking. Who'd want to stay in there with you juicers, I'd like to know?"

Owen interceded for his brother. "I believe that the point Cedric is trying to make, Mrs. Bookman, is that if you really have been in our house all evening, you can't possibly know if your husband is sleeping or even if at present he's actually in the cottage."

Silence underscored the accusatory thoughts everyone was surely harboring. I still wondered where Fairley had gone to, but Owen had more pressing matters. Though the mantel clock was showing four in the morning, he clapped his hands together and announced, "I want everyone to return to your rooms, get dressed, and come back down here as soon as you can. I have some important business regarding Mother to discuss with you all. Be quick about it."

Cedric and Charlotte exchanged furtive glances, presumably at the sharpness of Owen's tone.

"Owen sounds just like his mother, doesn't he?" Lucille whispered to me. "I told you so," she said and squeezed Oliver all the tighter.

* * *

The funereal atmosphere continued as we reconvened in the living room a quarter of an hour later. In our absence, Owen had gathered together a few sheets of paper. "Mother's new will," he announced when everyone was seated. "Written last night and witnessed by Mrs. Bookman and Aunt Lena."

"Last night?" someone whispered.

"You don't mean to tell us," Cedric charged, "that Mother died within hours of rewriting her will." That disturbing happenstance obviously raised questions, and Cedric appeared to be speaking for most everyone in the room.

Cedric and Charlotte continued their worried glances at each other, but I surmised that even Lena and Mrs. Bookman, the two legal witnesses to the will, had some reason for concern.

Owen raised his hand for silence. "Mother's words," he announced and then began to read: "'I, Muriel Laughton Cobb, being of sound mind and body—and at the same time worried for my life—do hereby leave all of my estate to my eldest child, Owen Lester Cobb, to be dispatched as he sees fit.'"

The response was predictable.

"All to you?" Cedric shouted at Owen. "Why all to you?"

"What did she mean—worried for her life?" Charlotte wanted to know.

Owen shook his head. "So quickly one forgets, eh, Charlotte? Do you not remember the arsenic in the sleeping draft Mother thought you had something to do with?"

"That's not fair," Charlotte shot back.

Owen smiled. "Oh, I think there's only one conclusion we can draw from Mother's last-minute revision of her will. Thanks to her discovery of the arsenic, I'm convinced our dear mother feared her life was in danger. I think she wanted to reassure herself. Don't you see? Leaving all to me was doubly helpful. Not only could she trust that her affairs would be in good hands, but she must also have believed that she was removing temptation from others."

"Bloody hell," muttered Cedric, "you can't be serious."

"I don't believe it," said Charlotte.

Oliver emitted a little bark.

"I was hoping I'd inherit a little something for myself," said Aunt Lena softly, "so I could move to Blackpool. I have a friend there who . . . ." She continued speaking, but her voice seemed to disappear, and I could hear no more of her plans.

Mrs. Bookman said nothing, but I'm sure that she had thoughts of her own about what her employer might have left to her and her husband for all their years of service.

Owen raised a forefinger to catch everyone's attention. "There's one more thing I should tell you all. Days ago, Mother informed me that she kept four-hundred pounds in bank notes locked in a drawer of her escritoire. Keen-eyed Mr. Garland has pointed out to me that a locked drawer in the desk has been broken into. When I looked inside it, I saw that the money was gone."

"Stolen?" Charlotte asked.

It was a question requiring no answer.

"What else is missing?" Cedric wanted to know.

"Mother's gold ring," Charlotte said, "the one with the serpents. It wasn't on her finger. I notice these things."

"What else?" Cedric demanded.

"I can't be certain," said Owen calmly, "but you can rest assured that I removed the most important paper—this one." And again, he held up the will.

"Important to *you maybe*," growled Cedric.

As Owen responded, he pointed at me. "I believe that everyone here—except, of course, my friend, Mr. Garland from America—he didn't know Muriel Cobb—had reason enough to want our mother dead." His glance traveled from person to person. "In a word, I believe she was murdered for that money."

"Murdered?" the word was whispered around the room.

"And just how do you know she was murdered?" Cedric asked. "She looked at peace to me."

Owen didn't answer that question. Instead, he announced, "According to Mrs. Bookman, her husband is asleep in their cottage. I shall go roust him from bed and send him into Haslemere to fetch the police. They should be here later today, and we shall soon get to the bottom of this horrible crime."

In a form of dismissal, Owen turned and began to walk away. Not to be denied, however, Charlotte intercepted him. While I couldn't hear what they were saying, Charlotte waved her arms about and stomped a foot. Then she turned around and with a dejected expression re-joined the group.

"I'm going for Bookman," Owen announced again, heading through the kitchen towards the rear door. "We need the police."

No one said anything once Owen had left. At least in the silence, you could tell that the rain had stopped.

Moments later, Lucille, still holding Oliver, walked out to the front porch. I followed soon after, and we stood in the darkness.

"You're the only one who's been exonerated, Ham," she said with a kind of desperation. "And you're leaving tomorrow—today, really. Isn't that right?"

I nodded. "That's my intention. Later this morning Doyle's man is supposed to be taking me to the train station in Haslemere."

"I must leave with you then. I can't stay here any longer. Even though Mother Cobb is gone, there's no hope for change."

"What do you mean?" I asked, finding myself once more in that uncomfortable situation positioned between husband and wife—not to mention the probability of the authorities' wanting to question Lucille as a suspect. As if to underscore my point, I thought I could hear Owen pounding on the door of Bookman's cottage in Owen's quest to summon the police. In fairness, I suppose I might simply have been hearing the rumble of distant thunder.

"Yesterday," Lucille said, "I told you that Charlotte had asked her mother for money to buy some costumes and go off to join her dance partner. Well, now that Owen is in charge, I just heard her ask him for the money. And her dear brother—my husband—said no. I tell you, Ham, I can't stay here any longer."

We stood in silence for the moment, but soon we heard footsteps on the wet gravel, and Owen turned the corner of the house and marched into view. Oliver raised his head at the arrival of his master, who was obviously returning from the Bookmans' cottage. Adroitly dodging the numerous puddles in his path, Owen stepped up onto the porch.

"Bookman's off to get the police," he said.

Whether Owen had heard Lucille's last words to me or not, I couldn't be certain, but seeing the two of us together like that in the dark seemed incriminating enough for the man.

"I say, Garland," he addressed me coolly, "friend or no, you're spending altogether too much time with my wife. In fact, though my mother—her mother-in-law—has just died, I shouldn't be surprised to hear Lucille tell me yet again that she'll be leaving Hearthstone with you."

Lucille looked frightened. Oliver let out a little cry as her eyes widened, and she shook her head. "No, Owen. That's not so. Why, I—I couldn't leave poor Oliver, could I?" She held up the dog as a kind of proof. "I'm staying here—with you and Oliver." And tightly hugging the dog who gave another cry, she went back into the house.

With a smirk, Owen shook his head, then marched through the doorway and up the stairs.

When it was my turn to go back in, I found Lucille seated at the empty table in the dining room still holding Oliver. A few plain crackers remained in a bowl, and she was feeding them to the dog. At the same time, she was tilting her head in the direction of the kitchen where I could now hear muffled voices arising. The softer one belonged to Mrs. Bookman. I didn't recognize the other.

I mouthed "Who?" to Lucille.

"Fairley," she mouthed back.

Ah, yes, the red-headed gamekeeper. Neither Lucille nor I could make out what was being said, so I put my forefinger to my lips to signal silence, and then I tiptoed closer to the kitchen door in order to listen in on the conversation.

"Mr. Owen may think my Norton is going for the police," Mrs. Bookman was saying, "but it wouldn't surprise me none if he just run off. He's been talking that way for a while."

"No," Fairley said, "'e'd never do such a thing. Why, me and 'im . . ."

His voice trailed off—as if he'd stopped himself from saying something—and Mrs. Bookman repeated suspiciously, "You and him—what?"

If an answer to the question were provided, I never heard it, for joining us at that moment in the dining room was Aunt Lena. Her eyes were red, as though she'd been crying.

"What's the matter, Lena?" Lucille asked as I walked back to the table.

"If only I had the money," she replied softly, "I'd be off to join my friend Hazel in Blackpool. But, you see, I can't afford the trip. I asked Muriel for it, but—well, you know how she was. 'No, Lena,' she said. 'If you can't afford to travel, it's God's way of telling you to stay where you are.'"

Lucille freed a hand from Oliver and patted Lena on the arm. "I'll ask Owen," she said. "I know he turned down a request from Charlotte, but he's always spoken so highly of you, Aunt Lena. I'm sure he'll be helpful. You'll see."

A sympathetic smile filled Lena's face. "Oh, Lucille," she said as warmly as seemed possible, "I already asked him. Just now, upstairs. Like his mother, there was no chaffering. He simply said no."

Lucille shook her head, apparently too tired to battle any longer. Indeed, we'd all been up most of the night. As far as I was concerned, there still remained an hour or so left to get some sleep.

Lucille climbed the stairs in front of me. She cradled Oliver tightly in her arms.

Monday Morning
May 8, 1899
Portsmouth Direct Line
(En route from Haslemere to London Waterloo)

Happy to put Hearthstone Hall behind me, I write these pages in the railway carriage during my return to London. It is still early in the day, and the events of the morning remain fresh in my mind.

By seven, I was eating Mrs. Bookman's simple breakfast of fried sole, toast, and jam. I had just finished my coffee when a knock on the rear door announced the arrival of Doyle's coachman and his trap, my transportation to the train station in Haslemere.

Here was my chance to leave. No authorities had arrived to say I couldn't, and discretion being the better part of valor (to quote Shakespeare in his native land), I figured I should take advantage of the opportunity.

Before setting out, I offered my farewells to everyone at Hearthstone, especially to Lucille. In fact, with my back to Owen, I made a point of raising my eyebrows questioningly to be certain that she still didn't plan on accompanying me. She shook her head with a regretful smile. I shrugged and placing my valise and frock coat in the trap, took my seat for the drive to Haslemere.

The beauty of a train ride!

The gentle sway of the carriage, the rhythmic clatter of the rails, the hypnotic panorama sweeping past the windows—in a word, the perfect setting for thought, for meditation, for contemplating what I was leaving behind: a collection of individuals one or more of whom might have wanted to see Muriel Cobb dead.

The police had failed to show up. The witnesses mistrusted one another. Did I think the authorities could properly sort out the details? In my head I could hear my father, my captain, calling for justice as he watched me leave the scene.

The beauty of a train ride!

Even as we approach Waterloo, there remains plenty of time for guilt to set in—but still enough time for me to have reached a decision.

Once the train arrives at the station, I shall hire a horse and cab to convey me to Baker Street. For recalling Doyle's advice about whom to seek in order to solve a mystery—"the world's first consulting detective," he called him—I shall deliver the relevant pages of this diary into the hands of Mr. Sherlock Holmes and let him decide for himself if the events I have recorded are deserving of further investigation.

Chapter Five

Watson's Narrative Resumed

> Hamlin was our star pitcher and was a good one.
> He threw the curves, and had one particularly effective sinker
> that had the big boys swinging wildly and missing.
> —Franklin Garland
> (Hamlin's brother)
> Letter to Eldon Hill
> July 19, 1940

Seldom have I seen Sherlock Holmes as enthusiastic as he was that late Monday morning upon setting down the pages from Hamlin Garland's diary. The author, who had been deservedly napping in a wing chair whilst we read his account, jerked awake at the sound of Holmes' voice.

"Well, well, Watson," my friend beamed, "it seems we have been presented with a classic murder mystery—the dead dowager empress and a collection of courtiers that might include a killer. Ah, Garland, you are awake. How fortunate!"

Holmes rubbed his hands together in eager anticipation. "My cases are at a lull at present—not much of interest since that nasty business with the blackmailer in January.* Though we must confirm Owen Cobb's claim that a crime has actually been committed, your diary describes just the sort of challenge I could use right now. What say you, friend Watson? Prepared to drop everything and follow the game to Hindhead?"

Fortunately, I had no patients to see that Monday, and I could easily arrange for a colleague to attend my surgery for the next day or two. "Count me in, Holmes," I said.

"And what about you, Garland? Are you willing to return to Hearthstone Hall?"

"In a word, yes," replied the American. "It would be unfaithful to my sense of justice—as well as to my father's—if I neglected to attempt to set matters straight."

"Excellent," said Holmes, replacing his pipe in the stand on the mantel. "Watson, secure a Gladstone for a night's stay in the country. Come, gentlemen, let us prepare ourselves to rusticate in Surrey."

It had just gone one. Within the half-hour, we were hailing a hansom in Baker Street and on our way to Waterloo. According to *Bradshaw*, the Portsmouth Direct, which called at Haslemere, was scheduled to depart at a quarter to three.

---

* Holmes refers to his encounter with Charles Augustus Milverton in the investigation involving Stephen Crane. Watson described the affair in *The Baron of Brede Place*.

Two hours later, beneath thick, grey clouds that added a sinister darkness to the land, a hired farm wagon conveyed us round the rim of the Devil's Punch Bowl to the manor house itself.

It was close to five o'clock when the wagon deposited us on the gravel before Hearthstone Hall, and a man with long, black hair whom I took to be Owen Cobb met us at the door. Clearly, he looked disappointed.

"Garland," he cried, his sharp tone revealing his annoyance, "what's all this about? I was expecting the arrival of the police, and instead I discover your unexpected return."

"The police aren't here yet?" Garland asked. "Bookman didn't raise them?"

"No, not yet." Cobb looked at Holmes and me. "And who might these gentlemen be?"

The American offered the introductions, explaining that we hoped to discover the true facts behind the death of Cobb's mother.

"Sherlock Holmes," Owen mused, running his fingers through his hair. "I've heard of you. Read some accounts of your cases, actually." Turning in my direction, he added, "Your reports are a bit too histrionic for my taste, Dr. Watson, but then I'm a poet by trade." With a wry smile, he added, "I should imagine that we poets spend more time pondering vocabulary than you crime-reporters do."

I chose to ignore the jibe. The man had just lost his mother; I could forgive him his trespasses.

Sherlock Holmes, however, cut straight to the quick. "If it is true, Mr. Cobb, that the authorities are on their way, I should very much like to see your mother's body before they arrive. The police have a way of corrupting such situations."

Cobb seemed to hesitate for just a moment, but then agreed and stepping aside, ushered the three of us into the house. "Upstairs," he said and pointed in the direction of the staircase.

With no butler present to take our accessories, I hung my bowler and mac on one of the hooks in the entry hall, and Holmes did the same with his deerstalker and Inverness. We placed our Gladstones on the floor beneath the coats, and Garland leant his valise against the wall next to our bags. Then we followed Cobb to the stairs.

It took but a moment to ascertain that Garland's diary had rightly characterised the Gothic atmosphere of the place—the gloom, the frowning portraits, the heavy furniture. Before I could absorb it all, however, we were intercepted by some of the very people about whom we had read in the American's diary.

From her blonde hair, I recognised Lucille Cobb. She was coming down the stairs with a greying older lady whom I took to be Lena, the sister of the dead woman. The corpulent young man who emerged from the dining room could only have been Cedric, and the sinewy young woman standing at the top of the stairs, his sister Charlotte.

"Is this the police, then?" Cedric asked.

"No," Owen said, pointing to my friend, "this is Sherlock Holmes, a private investigator." Turning towards me, he added, "And this is his associate, Dr. Watson. I know of their work, and based on their reputation, I have granted Mr. Holmes permission to examine Mother's room."

"If they're not the police," growled Cedric, "then I'm going out for a walk."

There were some grumblings among the others as well, but the reality of Mrs. Cobb's final decision to leave everything to her older son seemed to have invested the poet with a not-so-subtle aura of authority. Free from any significant resistance from the remaining personages, he led Holmes and me up the stairs to the bedroom belonging to the late Muriel Laughton Cobb.

From his waistcoat pocket, Cobb removed a brass key and unlocked the door. He was about to pass through the now open doorway, but Holmes held up an arm at the threshold to bar anyone but himself from entering.

"We must disturb the scene as little as possible," Holmes explained.

The curtains were open, and enough daylight was left to illuminate the entire chamber. From my vantage point at the doorway, I could see the deceased in her bed. In contrast to the darkness of all the black-mahogany wood surrounding her—the bed's tall headboard and footboard; its side table; a large, double-doored armoire; a low-slung chest of drawers with bottles of perfume and the like, and a stately *escritoire*—Muriel Cobb rested as peacefully as Garland had described her.

She lay on her back beneath a white quilt, her head raised slightly on a white pillow, her grey hair fixed in a pair of long plaits. Her eyes were closed, her face relaxed, a white lace collar secured round her neck. Her arms lay cloaked in the sleeves of her cream-coloured night dress. Like Garland, I echo the Bard: Death's pale flag had not yet advanced.

"No one has touched her?" Holmes called to Cobb at the door.

"I pushed up her sleeve to check her pulse," he said. "The wrist without the *serviette*."

"The wrist without the cut from dinner, I presume," said Holmes.

Cobb raised his eyebrows in surprise.

"We read Garland's notes," my friend explained.

Owen Cobb turned to stare at the American standing next to him. "I had no idea, Garland. I can only wonder how much more you wrote down."

"Anything else touched?" Holmes queried.

Owen explained that he had extinguished the lamp and closed the window.

Thus informed, Sherlock Holmes commenced his investigation. With no hesitation, he carefully turned down the high collar of the dead woman's night dress. Though I may be a doctor, no medical licence was required to recognise the red oval marks that had been concealed by the lace collar covering the woman's throat. I had seen such malicious evidence in other cases—tell-tale imprints from the fingers that doubtlessly strangled the life out of the poor woman.

"Murder," I said to myself, whilst witnessing at the same moment the unforgettable look of astonishment on the face of Owen Cobb.

Moving away from the bed, Holmes proceeded to inspect the surroundings. First, he approached the window and, dropping to his knees, scrutinised the water marks on the pale carpet where the rain had come in. Then he raised the sash and the glazing and peered at the sill, both inside the room and the ledge facing outdoors. Next, he noted the dresser whose drawers he withdrew and whose interiors he examined. He did likewise with the *escritoire,* paying specific attention to the facing with the jemmied lock.

"The drawer from which the money was taken," Holmes said to Cobb.

"Indeed," came the reply. "I hadn't noticed the break-in at first. As you can see, the scratches are scarcely visible, but Garland pointed them out to me. Mother had four hundred pounds in bank notes in that drawer, and now they are missing. As for her official papers—the will and such—those were untouched, and I removed them myself."

Holmes now focused his attention on the large armoire. He examined its left-hand door in particular, indicating to us a near-vertical crack running down two-thirds of its height. My friend drew his forefinger slowly along the split and after opening both doors, shuffled through the collection of dark dresses hanging within. Rather surprisingly, he then proceeded to bend his tall frame downward, step inside the compartment, and shut the doors.

Cobb and Garland looked to me for an explanation, but I could only shrug before Holmes emerged a few moments later.

Saved for last was Holmes' inspection of the table on the far side of the bed. Just as Garland had described in his diary, upon a white doily next to the Brontë novel—*Jane Eyre,* to be precise—stood a pitcher of water, a glass, and a clear bottle of pills. This last he picked up to scrutinise.

"Potassium bromide," Cobb volunteered from the doorway, "to help Mother sleep."

Holmes nodded and lifting the bottle, removed the stopper and sniffed the contents. Then he withdrew a single grey pill and ran it across his tongue. With a dramatic frown, he walked to the door where I was standing, handed a pill to me, and requested that I also sample it.

I immediately recognised the slightly vinegary smell. The bitter taste confirmed my opinion. "Not potassium bromide," I said. "It is morphine."

"My thought exactly," said Holmes. Turning to Cobb, he announced, "It would appear from the evidence, Mr. Cobb, that your initial conclusion was quite correct. Unhappily, your mother's death was anything but natural. The unfortunate woman was first drugged and then strangled—a clear case of murder."

Owen Cobb placed his hand on the doorknob for stability, then shut his eyes a moment. Consistent with Garland's report in his diary, the poet stated simply, "Just as I feared."

Under the circumstances, there was not much else to say, and Garland, Holmes, and I looked to Owen Cobb for any additional reaction. But such was not to be, for all at once, Charlotte's shrill voice echoed throughout the house.

"It's Cedric," she hollered from the foot of the stairs. "He's shouting for help. There's been an accident out at the Drop."

Chapter Six

An Array of Suspects

> I have all the prejudices of an old cricketer, and yet I cannot get away from the fact that baseball is the better game. . . . It has many points which make it the ideal game both for players and spectators.
> —Arthur Conan Doyle
> *Our Second American Adventure*

As a doctor, I had no choice but to answer Charlotte's call. Holmes, Cobb, and Garland trailed after me as I rushed down the stairs and out the front door onto the gravel. A blast of cold air struck me, and under the darkening sky, I followed Charlotte towards the Punch Bowl, wondering all the while what had happened, who was hurt.

With the three others not far behind, I trailed her through the brush and down a precipitous path that I presumed would end at the base of Demon's Drop, the dangers of which Garland had already informed us. Charlotte knew her way and maneuvered dexterously down the steep trail whilst I tripped over the odd tree root and stumbled through the thick overgrowth that reached out into the path.

Suddenly, even Charlotte pulled up short; upon the dirt before her lay a two-foot-long brown adder. No doubt disturbed by our heavy footfalls, it darted into the brush with a whiplike snap of its zigzag-patterned back.

I had no time to worry about venomous snakes, however, for at the foot of a formation of sand-coloured rocks just beyond Charlotte, I spied the thick-set form of Cedric Cobb. He was kneeling over a broken body, its left arm and right leg twisted in unnatural angles, the ginger hair helping identify the poor fellow about whom we had read in Garland's diary.

"Andrew Fairley," Cedric confirmed when I reached him. "Our gamekeeper. He must have fallen."

With a frown, Charlotte stared up at the top of the cliff towering above us.

At the same time, I waved Cedric away from the body and climbed awkwardly over the rocks to reach it. When I did, I felt Fairley's neck for a pulse. Not only did I find none, but I could clearly discern his fractured skull. I looked at Cedric and Charlotte and shook my head. "He's dead," I told them. "The fall killed him."

Holmes, Garland, and Owen Cobb arrived in time to hear my verdict.

"I have to agree with you, Doctor," said Owen who, like Charlotte, cast his eyes upward to the top of the cliff. "As much as he drank, he must have lost his balance up there."

"What are you saying, Owen?" Charlotte cried, clearly nettled. "Fairley was too sure-footed to have fallen. The man knew his way about—even when drunk. It happened often enough."

Holmes leant in next to me. "Be a good fellow," he whispered in my ear. "Keep the others distracted whilst I have a look at the body."

Holmes and I exchanged positions. I climbed down from the rocks; he climbed up. I knew him well enough to understand that he wanted time to examine the body on his own—free from people gawping at a second corpse within twenty-four hours.

Once I saw Holmes turn his back to me and crouch over the dead gamekeeper, I shepherded away the onlookers. When we had moved far enough from Holmes to assure his privacy, I asked them what they could tell me concerning Fairley's responsibilities about the house and how well he carried them out.

"Fairley's responsibilities?" Cedric repeated. "He fed the animals—the pigs, the chickens, our two horses."

"He drank too much," Owen stated for a second time. "Not too difficult to imagine him stumbling over the edge."

Charlotte shook her head though offered no words in support of the dead gamekeeper.

Garland simply shrugged. "I didn't know the poor fellow. I only saw him attend to the trap horse that brought me here."

And overheard him talking to Mrs. Bookman about some mystery with her husband, I recalled. It made perfect sense for Garland not to bring up that discussion.

Indeed, Cedric seemed to be the man's only supporter. "Fairley was a good mate," he said with what appeared to be a nostalgic smile, "at least, when it came to supplying us with whisky. He was best at that job. I had to pass him the money to buy it, of course, but I have a bit saved for just such occasions."

Like last night, I could not help thinking, *the night of your mother's murder. Drunk with your mates, Cedric? Or perhaps the foundation of a convincing alibi.*

"Well, I for one never trusted the man," Owen said sharply. "When he wasn't drunk, he was scheming ways to get more money. I never knew why Mother kept him on."

Heated feelings to the contrary, people were shivering in the cold—we had all run out so quickly at Charlotte's call that no one had stopped for an overcoat. Still, the spectre of Holmes and the dead body seemed alluring enough to keep them standing by if only at a distance, stomping their feet and opening and closing their fingers to increase circulation.

"Nothing more to do here," Holmes said at last. "Let us return to the house." To Owen and Cedric, he added, "We can't leave the body out here in the wilds. Perhaps, you two gentlemen will be good enough to transport Mr. Fairley's remains back to his rooms."

Charlotte took the lead whilst Owen and his brother lifted the deceased—Owen at the head, Cedric at the feet. With Holmes, Garland, and me following, the two brothers, breathing deeply, managed to carry the dead gamekeeper back up the steep path and across the flagstone courtyard. Upon entering the small alcove attached to the stables where Fairley had resided, they laid out the corpse on the bed.

"We need the police—a coroner, actually," I insisted to Owen Cobb when the brothers had finished with the body.

Cobb shook his head. "Early this morning I sent our butler to Haslemere to get the constable. I can't imagine what's happened."

"You need to send someone else," Holmes joined in. "So far, there have been two mysterious deaths here. As Watson has informed you, the authorities must be notified."

"I'll go," said Hamlin Garland.

"No," said Owen, "no one knows you here. The police will think you're just some mad Yank. I'll go myself in the morning. There's no need to hurry. The two people are already dead." He paused a moment, then added, "Sorry, if that sounded a bit unfeeling."

Sherlock Holmes stated the case: "At least one of those two people, your mother—and possibly both—has been murdered. Let us not forget that whoever committed the fatal act must still be here among us."

"Sorry," said Owen, seemingly unperturbed, "it's just about time for dinner. Let me tell Mrs. Bookman that the two of you and my American friend are staying the night at the Hall. We'll tell everyone to be on their guard, and I'll bring the police here on the morrow."

Holmes shrugged assent. With no immediate solution to the crimes in sight, Owen's suggestion to return to the routines of Hearthstone Hall seemed a reasonable plan. Yet I was sure that Holmes joined me in recognizing that Owen's offer to fetch the police was double-edged.

Oh, the offer seemed helpful enough on the surface, but Owen's desire to solve the mystery might also be a dodge to suggest his innocence. No one would possibly expect the murderer himself to summon the police to the scene of his crime—no one, that is, except some doubting Thomas who might suspect such a villain of creating the false impression of inculpability.

Cedric went up to his room, leaving Garland, Holmes and myself with Owen. It took but a moment for Owen to secure a trio of small glasses. "The sherry is on the table between the chairs, gentlemen," he told us. "Feel free to indulge. Pray, excuse me whilst I inform Mrs. Bookman of our additional guests."

Owen departed for the kitchen, and Holmes, explaining that he had some problems he hoped to clear up, headed for the entry hall. Upon seeing him disappear among the jackets, I sat down in one of the wing chairs, Garland in the other. It was the American who poured our sherry from the crystal decanter situated between us.

Garland and I had but a few moments to savour our drinks before Lena entered the room and took the couch opposite.

"Sherry?" I offered, holding up the decanter.

"No thank you," she said and clasped her hands together in her lap. "Not to speak ill of the dead," she smiled sadly, "but my sister was a difficult woman." She paused to look left and right as if to be certain she would not be overheard. "She'd been such even as a child. We were always at odds, Muriel and I. Usually, it was over something of mine that she wanted—my dolls, my clothes, my jewellery. But my *fiancé* is the best example—and the most painful."

"What do you mean?" Garland asked.

"Why, Muriel stole my man—a rich fellow, he was—Alexander Cobb—you'll recognise the surname. She won him away from me with her wily charm. They married and had the three children you've already met. Not long after Cedric was born, their father was killed in a riding accident in the Devil's Punch Bowl. His horse stumbled over a tree root. Fell on top of poor Alex. Broke his neck.

"Muriel inherited everything. Worse, she came to appreciate her skills at manipulating, and over the years she worked hard at converting her children into younger versions of herself. What I really mean, of course, is the darker side of herself. She turned Charlotte and Cedric into selfish, egotistical money-grubbers, and ever since she orchestrated Owen's return to Hearthstone, he's taken over the authoritarian role that Muriel had assumed for so long. As much as I hate to say it, so desperate had each of the children become for their inheritance that, given the right circumstances, I believe any one of the three capable of murdering their mother."

I cocked an eyebrow. "Certainly," I said to her, "the situation can't be that bad."

Just then, loud footfalls could be heard thumping their way down the stairs.

"Shame on me," Lena murmured. "I'm afraid I've said too much." With those words, she got up and hurriedly left the room.

"I reckon," Garland smiled wryly, "we were just given the names of three possible suspects. "Cedric, Charlotte and Owen—all of the Cobb children."

"Unless Lena was trying to put us on the wrong scent," I replied, as suspicious of the woman now as I had been of Owen earlier.

The loud footfalls belonged to Cedric. Entering the room moments after Lena's exit, he ambled towards the couch and sat down heavily in the same spot that she had just vacated. The stout young man stretched out both his arms along the top of the cushioned backrest and uttered a long sigh. Then he said, "I noticed Aunt Lena talking to you both. I shouldn't be surprised to learn that she was blaming my brother or sister—or even me, come to that—for killing our mother. No, it wouldn't surprise me at all."

"And should we believe her?" I asked.

"Dr. Watson," he chuckled drily, "you would not ask such a question if you had the information concerning Aunt Lena that I do." Beneath his curls, he smiled broadly, not unlike a child who has a secret that he is longing to reveal.

"And just what information is that, my good man?"

Rather than answering my question, Cedric got up to retrieve a glass. He then procured the decanter from the table, poured himself a sherry, and returned to his seat. With great deliberation, he raised the glass towards us in a silent toast and drank.

Only then did he speak. "No one besides me seemed to notice," said he, "but I assure you that last night, after we learned that Mother was dead, something curious occurred. Owen brought Aunt Lena down the stairs. He told us he'd found her cowering inside her armoire—well, we all know how frightened she is of lightning and thunder, don't we? Ever since she was a little girl."

"Yes," I said impatiently, "we're all quite familiar with her phobia. Get to the point, if you'd be so kind."

"What do you suppose?" Cedric blurted, "Her hair was wet!"

"And just what is that supposed to prove?" Garland wanted to know.

"Why," Cedric smirked, "it proves she was out in the rain last night." He shook his head at our obvious obtuseness.

"And were her clothes equally wet?" I asked. "They certainly should have been if your surmise is correct."

"Well, no," admitted Cedric. "But she was wearing a dressing gown—she could have changed into it."

"Perhaps she had washed her hair," Garland suggested.

I sipped some sherry to consider the matter, then asked, "Why is it necessary to convince us that she was out in the rain?"

Cedric reached for the decanter and refilled his glass. He drank some more before answering. "Because I believe," he said, "I believe Aunt Lena strangled her sister. If you accept all that muck about her fear of storms, then I think the lightning bolt must have struck that tree when she was in Mother's room and frightened Aunt Lena so badly that she went running into Mother's armoire for shelter and hid there till she felt it safe to come out.

"When she gained the courage to emerge, she discovered that the bedroom door had been locked from the outside—we have Owen to thank for that—and so in spite of the storm that so frightened her, in order to get back to her own bed, she climbed out the window onto the balcony, which she traversed back to her room."

"An intriguing theory," I said. "Rest assured that I shall share it with Sherlock Holmes."

Cedric smiled. His mission apparently accomplished, he played with a loose curl near his ear.

At the same time, Garland and I looked knowingly at each other. By now we had heard a number of stories, and I could only assume that the American and I were in agreement—too many suspects presenting accusations against one another—and all of them members of the same scheming family.

Chapter Seven

The Meeting in the Sitting Room

> You must be prepared
> to have the situation misinterpreted
> and be able to protect yourself adequately.
> —Garland Lord
> *Murder's Little Helper*

With her husband gone for the police, not only did Charity Bookman have to prepare the Monday-night meal, but she also had to serve it. Such a challenge resulted in her running to and fro, first out of the kitchen and then back into it, her hands laden with full serving dishes or used platters. However noble, her efforts resulted in a bland affair of boiled chicken and roasted potatoes, evoking little reaction from the collection of silent diners seated at the table.

Once we had finished Mrs. Bookman's custard, Sherlock Holmes rose. "Let us adjourn to the sitting room. It is time to review what we have learned about the mysterious deaths of the last twenty-four hours."

Lena, a possible suspect herself, surprised me by saying, "What a wonderful idea." She took Charlotte by the hand, and the two of them settled themselves on the couch as if they were in a theatre. Cedric occupied one of the wing chairs, and Owen pulled up a wooden bow-back that stood against the wall. Cradling Oliver, whom she had carried down from the bedroom, Lucille joined Garland on a wooden settee. Even as Mrs. Bookman cleared the dishes from the table, she too lent an ear to our proceedings. I took over a tufted leather ottoman, which I had rolled within a few feet to the left of where Holmes was standing.

From the start, I sensed a curious mixture of feelings among the assembled residents of Hearthstone Hall. It seemed obvious that the demise of Muriel Cobb had concocted a veritable stew of conflicting emotions. Grief and joy, suspicion and fear—they permeated the sitting room that evening. Sadness at the loss of the matriarch competed with the exhilaration born from the end of her authoritarian rule. But though a sense of freedom was continuing to build, the compelling question of who, like Mother Cobb and Fairley, might be the next to die engendered understandable anxiety.

Sherlock Holmes began the meeting by holding up two folded sheets of paper, one in each hand. "Owen furnished me with both of Mrs. Cobb's wills, the old and the new. The earlier will is a formal document." As he spoke, he displayed it to the group. "It divides the entire estate equally among Mrs. Cobb's three children. It also sets aside an additional stipend for her sister as well as for the butler and cook and for the gamekeeper, recently deceased. The will was formally witnessed by one Ebenezer Falwell, a solicitor, and by Matthew Redding, his clerk."

Sighs and murmurs passed among the listeners as they contemplated what might have been.

"But then, as you all now know, Mrs. Cobb changed her mind. Apparently, in the initial months of Owen's work here, his mother discovered how well he performed his responsibilities—not to mention the authoritarian manner so much like her own with which he carried them out. Presumably, it was during this period that she decided to leave her entire estate to him. She must have concluded that Owen would know how to manage the money as well as the grounds and, just as important, be able to keep Charlotte and Cedric in line."

"Rubbish," muttered Cedric.

"The new will"—and here Holmes held high the other paper—"was witnessed by Muriel Cobb's sister Lena Laughton and Mrs. Charity Bookman."

All eyes focused upon Lena.

"I know, I know," she said simply, "I was witnessing my own exclusion. But Muriel said it had to be done. Why cause a row? I believe Mrs.

Bookman felt the same. She was upstairs at the moment Muriel sought another witness, and if one truly stops to consider, most every one of us always found it so much easier to agree with Muriel than to do otherwise."

Heads nodded round the room.

"Let one not forget, however," Holmes said, "that in this second will, in addition to expressing her new desires for distribution, Mrs. Cobb also wrote that she was fearful for her life."

"That was due to the poison she discovered in her sleeping medication," Owen explained.

"The green substance," Garland added.

"Mother blamed Charlotte," said Cedric. "She accused Charlotte of mixing up her bottles or some such thing."

"I did not," Charlotte said firmly.

They sounded like school children tattling on one another.

"Unfortunately," said Owen, "Mother threw the bottle into the hearth. It shattered, and thus we will never know the truth."

Oliver, the little terrier, chose the moment to emit a soft but lengthy whine as he resettled himself in Lucille's arms.

For his part, Sherlock Holmes smiled briefly and putting down the papers he was holding, extracted a white handkerchief from an inner pocket.

"I took the liberty of examining some of those glass fragments," he said. Then, with great deliberateness, he proceeded to unfold his linen and between thumb and forefinger carefully pick out a tiny shard of clear glass perhaps a quarter of an inch square and hold it high for all to see. It appeared to be coated in green.

"It's green," announced Charlotte needlessly, for we all could observe the colour. "Just as we said."

"Even from where I'm sitting," observed Cedric, "you can detect the arsenic."

Holmes responded with another quick smile. "In the late-eighteenth century, a Swedish chemist called Carl Wilhelm Scheele, developed a strikingly beautiful green pigment for paint. Despite its aesthetic appeal, the pigment was eventually discovered to contain copper arsenite, a highly poisonous compound, a highly poisonous *green* compound. Ever since, people have feared what they call 'Scheele's green.'"

"So, Mother Cobb was right to throw out the green medication," said Lucille. "It could have killed her."

"Not quite," countered Holmes. "Scheele's legacy has given the colour green a bad name; as a result, many safe compounds of that colour have been mistakenly considered dangerous."

"It's not the colour that poses the threat," said Garland.

"Correct," agreed Holmes. "As it happens, I have written a monograph on the nature of inks. No need for chemical analyses tonight, but I can assure you that the green substance in your mother's sleeping potion was nothing more than standard ink containing a greenish hue—umber green, actually, almost grey—ink that most usually can be found in the tiny inner chamber of a fountain pen or in a much larger inkwell atop someone's writing desk. In a word, the potion in Mrs. Cobb's medication was completely harmless. It was merely intended to look ominous."

Charlotte breathed a sigh of relief.

"Mrs. Cobb didn't know it was harmless, of course," Holmes went on, "and in fact, her discovery of the green substance made her draw the conclusion—not an illogical one, as it turned out—that someone wanted to kill her."

"But why go to the bother of pouring green ink into a bottle of medicine she might not even use?" asked Charlotte.

Holmes offered a quick response. "The villain needed to be certain that your mother would take the pills and not the liquid. He—or she— turned the liquid the colour of arsenic to frighten your mother. That way, she would be forced to rely on what she thought was potassium bromide pills, but what was in fact tablets of morphine."

"But why would anyone do such a thing?" Charlotte asked. "There's no point. We've been written out of our inheritance."

"Not all of us," growled Cedric.

Owen surveyed the room. "I hope no one is accusing *me*. I didn't put Mother up to writing a new will."

Cedric and Charlotte exchanged suspicious looks. I am certain they did not trust their brother who now, for whatever the reason, was standing up and facing his aunt.

"I'd like to know," Owen said defiantly, "what Aunt Lena was doing prowling about upstairs before our mother was—how did you put it, Mr. Holmes?—'drugged and strangled.' I was downstairs, and I looked up and saw her."

Lena again, I thought. *First Cedric, now Owen—both nephews determined to implicate their aunt.*

"Why, Owen," Lena replied "you know how I am with storms. I'm not proud of my childish behaviour, but I was so frightened that I couldn't sleep. Expecting Muriel's tablets to have already put her to sleep, I went into her room to get one for myself from the bottle she keeps by her bed. She appeared to be sleeping—though now we know the horrible truth—so I quietly took a tablet and went back to my room."

Owen shook his head. "Only because you're my dear mother's sister am I not calling you a liar."

"Owen!" Lena exclaimed.

Owen ran his hand through his thick hair. "Lucille had requested that I sleep down here, so when I heard someone moving about—you, as it turned out, Aunt Lena—I moved to the bottom of the staircase and saw you in the upstairs hall on your way to Mother's room. I waited many minutes, but I never saw you exit. In fact, I didn't see you again until I found you quaking in the armoire in your own room. I have no idea what went on up there, but it all seems very suspicious to me."

"I'll tell you what seems suspicious to *me*, Aunt Lena," Cedric said as Owen resumed his seat. "Your wet hair. I suppose now is as good a time as any to ask why your hair was wet when you came down the stairs with Owen. I've already told Dr. Watson about it."

I nodded confirmation whilst Lena merely shook her head.

"Here's what I think happened," Cedric said in answer to his own question. "I think you got trapped in Mother's room after you killed her. I believe that once Owen locked Mother's door, you were forced to make your escape in the rain out the window and along the balcony."

Silence followed the young man's accusation.

Lena's eyes filled with tears. "Oh, Cedric," she said, "how can you even say such a thing? We had our differences, but Muriel was my sister."

"She was my mother!" Cedric shot back.

"Mine too," said Charlotte.

"Mine as well," added Owen.

Lena looked at each of the three and wiped a tear from her red-rimmed eyes. "All right then," she said, clasping her hands together, "I see I must explain."

Everyone, her niece and nephews in particular, leant forward, the better to hear Lena's words.

"You're quite correct, Owen. I did go to Muriel's room, just as you said. But not for the sleeping tablets. I'm ashamed to say that, though I didn't have a specific plan in mind, I had the expectation that her tablets had done their work and I could steal her money without disturbing her."

Silence again until Owen stated what seemed to be the obvious: "So, you're the one who robbed our mother."

Lena shook her head. "No, nephew, I'm not. For whilst I did see Muriel sleeping peacefully—at least, I thought she was asleep at the time—I also saw that the desk drawer had been broken into and that the money I sought was gone. Someone had been there before me."

Cedric muttered some indistinguishable sound of disbelief. Owen merely smirked.

"There was no point in staying in the room any longer, but just as I was about to leave, that lightning bolt struck the tree with a horrific clap, and as embarrassed as I am to admit it, I was so terrified that I bolted into Muriel's armoire and pulled the doors closed behind me."

Though Cedric and Owen shook their heads in reaction to Lena's explanation, Sherlock Holmes corroborated her story. "You pushed back the clothes in the armoire to make room for yourself," he observed, at the same time withdrawing from his pocket a narrow strand of red fabric. "Somehow, you lost this hair-ribbon, which I found upon the floor inside the armoire."

Instinctively, Lena reached to the back of her grey hair even though another red ribbon now held it together. "I should imagine so," she shrugged. "When I came out, I believed that Muriel was still sleeping. I just wanted to return to my own room, and I tiptoed to the door in order to leave. But it was locked—by Owen I have since learned—and so I got up all my courage to face the storm, which had lessened a bit after the thunder clap.

"I managed to climb out the window and onto the balcony. By then, much to my relief, it was only a thin rain falling. I got back to my room through a French window and changed into a dry dressing gown. But before I could take a towel to my hair, more thunder exploded, and I hid in my own armoire until Owen came in and rescued me."

"I appreciate your honesty," Holmes said. "It is always difficult to admit one's fears, especially in so public a forum."

"Thank you, Mr. Holmes," said Lena. "But it should not be too difficult within the confines of a loving family."

She spoke so directly that I detected not a hint of sarcasm.

"But now," Lena said, turning to face Cedric, "I'd like to pose a question of my own. I'd like to ask Cedric what *he* was planning when I ran into him in the hall before Owen discovered Muriel's death."

Cedric sat up straight. "I—I heard people moving about," said he. "I came out of my room to see what was going on."

Holmes interrupted the exchange. "Do you recall," he asked Lena, "if Cedric's room was dark, or was there light inside?"

The grey-haired woman bit her lip as she puzzled over the question. "Dark, I believe."

"In which case," said Holmes, "I suggest to you that Cedric was coming *up* the stairs. If he was just popping out to see what was happening beyond his room, his lamp would still be lighted."

"All right, all right," said Cedric, raising both hands. "If we're all admitting what we're embarrassed about, I suppose it's my turn now. Yes, I was indeed coming *up* the stairs. I was returning from Bookman's cottage. I'd been drinking with him and Fairley. In fact, I was drunk enough that Bookman had to help me back to the house. Maybe it was the whisky that gave me the courage, but I decided it was time to ask Mother for money, so I could finally leave this place."

"It's true," Charlotte said. "Now that I think about it, I heard him go to Mother's room. He knocked and said, 'It's Cedric, Mother.'"

"Thank you, sister," Cedric smiled. "As it turned out, there was no answer, so I went to my own room. No point in announcing to all of you that I was seeking to enter a bedroom where a murder had been committed."

Cedric's explanation sounded reasonable. Yet I could not help wondering why on that night of all nights he had sought out his mother.

As if reading my mind, he said, "I am compelled to point out before anyone asks that, had I been the one who stole Mother's money, there would be no reason in the world to be going to her room to ask for some."

Amidst a host of murmurs, Holmes took centre stage again. From his pocket he produced a shiny gilt button, which he held up for the group to see. Even the dog, attracted to the reflection of candlelight, raised his head.

"I found this button in the hand of the dead man, Fairley, when I examined his body yesterday. It would appear to have been torn from the coat of his assailant—of his killer, I should say, for its discovery most conclusively suggests he was pushed to his death."

"Another murder," Lena gasped.

"Earlier," Holmes continued, "I inspected the jackets and coats hanging on the hooks near the entry hall and discovered a pea jacket that was missing just such a button."

"Mine," admitted Cedric, quickly adding, "but I haven't worn it in days."

"There was a fragrance about the coat," Holmes said, "a hint of lavender."

Cedric raised both hands again and shook his head. "Not mine," he grinned.

"Aunt Lena wears lavender perfume," Charlotte said.

"So do I on occasion," volunteered Lucille. "In fact, I had some on when Ham and I toured the Devil's Punch Bowl yesterday afternoon. My word, it seems so long ago. What's more, I was wearing Cedric's pea coat."

Though Lucille seemed to have settled the matter, Lena said, "I gave a bottle of lavender perfume to Mrs. Bookman."

"Leave Charity out of it," Charlotte exclaimed.

"'*Charity*' is it now?" Owen shot back.

Charlotte balled her hands into fists. "Charity Bookman has been more than kind to me. Not only has she made dance costumes of the finest quality as I requested—that's what she was doing in my room the other night—but she has also given me money so I can resume my dancing career. Charity is a most generous soul indeed."

The mention of her name brought Mrs. Bookman into the sitting room.

"Where did you get the money you gave to Charlotte, Mrs. Bookman?" Owen wanted to know.

"It is my life savings, Mr. Owen," the cook said. "I stole nothing—if that's what you're hinting at. Miss Charlotte is a wonderful dancer, and I want her to have every opportunity to succeed. I helped raise her, don't you forget, Mr. Owen, just as I done for *you*. And for Mr. Cedric too, I might add."

Suddenly, no one had anything more to say. Major and minor guilt often produces such a result.

It was Lucille who put an end to the discussion. She had said little during the evening, but now voiced a relevant concern. "Where are the police? Without them, nothing will be decided." She looked round the room at all of us. With a disappointed shrug, she announced, "It's been a very long day. I'm taking Oliver upstairs and going to bed."

Mrs. Bookman showed Holmes and me to our respective chambers, and we too, along with all the others, retired for the night.

Chapter Eight

The Arrival of Scotland Yard

> We don't play that much [football] in the West.
> We go in more for baseball. More science.
> —Hamlin Garland
> *Boy Life on the Prairie*

*T*hough comforting, it would be naive to assume that the Monday-night discussion had relieved the anxiety among the Cobbs. At first, Holmes and I were the only attendees at table early Tuesday morning. Almost immediately, however, Garland joined us, and once Mrs. Bookman had presented a breakfast of kippers and toast, Cedric entered wearing a pair of tinted eye-glasses. With the heavens still slate-grey, the darkened spectacles were no doubt simply for show. In any case, the four of us were soon silently drinking our coffees.

Suddenly, Charlotte burst into the dining room and in a paroxysm of anger slammed a golden ring down on the table. I recognised the ring immediately from Garland's description in his diary:

a pair of entwined serpents, their heads separated by an oval-shaped ruby.

"What's this then?" Cedric asked, removing his darkened lenses.

Charlotte held up the ring. "*This*," she exclaimed, "belonged to Mother, and *this* is what I found at the bottom of the trunk in *your* room, brother. After hearing about your button turning up in Fairley's dead hand, I decided you are not to be trusted. I waited by your room for you to come down to breakfast, and then in I went and searched."

"You searched my room?"

"Indeed, I did—and a good thing too. Otherwise, we would never have known about your theft of Mother's ring."

Cedric stared at the object lying on the table. "But I—I don't know how it got there," he stammered. "I—"

"You what?" said Owen, striding into the room. Attired in his tweed Norfolk shooting jacket, a plaid muffler round his neck, he repeated to Cedric, "You what?"

Charlotte pointed at the piece of gold jewellery. "I found Mother's ring in his room," she proclaimed. "That proves—"

"It doesn't prove anything," said Cedric.

"Mother's ring, you say," Owen repeated. He picked it up and turning it round and round, carefully examined the thing for a full minute or so.

"Well," he said at last, thrusting the ring into his coat pocket, "we'll just have to wait and see, won't we?"

With a look of disgust, Cedric replaced his dark glasses and returned to his coffee.

For his part, Owen had other concerns. Tugging at his lapels to be certain his jacket fit smoothly, he turned to my friend. "I'm off to Haslemere, Mr. Holmes. To fetch the police—as promised. Maybe *they* can get to the bottom of all this, including—" here he cocked an eyebrow in his brother's direction—"what Cedric has been up to with Mother's ring."

Behind his glasses, Cedric frowned.

In preparation for his departure, Owen leant over Charlotte's shoulder, requisitioned a piece of toast, and took a bite.

Just as he was about to leave, however, we heard a carriage roll up the narrow passageway to the house. Given the drama of the previous twenty-four hours, all of us must certainly have been pondering the identity of this visitor, for as soon as the horses came to a halt, the six of us at table hastened to the outer door to see who it was that had arrived.

Owen was the first to speak. "No drive to Haslemere for me," he observed, for much to the relief or consternation of all of us, on the gravel stood a police four-wheeler. What is more, a familiar visage—at least, to Holmes and me—peered out of its window. From above portly pouches, the twinkling eyes of Scotland Yard Inspector Athelney Jones surveyed the scene.

Attentive readers may recall that, though Holmes had worked with the man many years before in the Bishopgate jewel case, my first introduction to the round-faced inspector came in the investigation related to the murder of Bartholomew Sholto. Even so, in the account I titled *The Sign of Four* it was not the inspector nor even the deadly blowgun wielded by Tonga, the Andaman Islander, whom I most remember. On the contrary, it was during the Sholto investigation that I met the lovely Mary Morstan, the charming woman who was to become my wife for the few short years she had left on this earth.

Let me say from the start that Athelney Jones never inspired confidence. Holmes included him in his list of Yarders (like Lestrade and Gregson) that he regarded as "out of their depths." In addition to the inspector's missteps in the Sholto murder, one may recall the role of Athelney Jones in the cases I recently recorded as "The Problem of the Half-Smoked Trichinopoly" and "The Adventure of the Stolen Dark-Lantern"—neither one of which, I am afraid, proved the man to be the most insightful of detectives.

On this occasion, however, there appeared reasonable hope for better results. For as the heavy inspector lowered himself out of the four-wheeler, it was clear that Athelney Jones had an assistant.

Joining the inspector in his walk across the gravel was a sharp-eyed, uniformed constable. What is more, the latter was steering in our direction a manacled and dejected older man whom the Cobb siblings instantly recognised.

"Bookman!" Owen shouted.

The irony was inescapable. The very fellow whom Owen had told us he'd sent to fetch the police was returning with them in their custody.

Mrs. Bookman had apparently been watching from a front window when the four-wheeler arrived as she now came running out to see her husband.

Before the constable could make a move, the woman slapped Bookman across the face. "You dog!" she exclaimed. "Where have you been?"

Reacting as quickly as he could, the constable stepped between husband and wife. Charlotte came forward, and placing an arm on Mrs. Bookman's shoulder, helped her back away.

"I say," observed Athelney Jones, "here's a nasty reception. And right at its centre, Mr. Sherlock Holmes."

"I expect nothing less than such excitement," Holmes replied drily, "upon the arrival of a representative of Scotland Yard."

"Quite right," observed Athelney Jones, interpreting, as I am certain my friend anticipated, Holmes' sarcasm as a compliment. The inspector then regarded the people who had come from the house. "What a menagerie, eh, Mr. Holmes? A woman dead, I am told. This man—" he jerked his head in the direction of the fettered Bookman— "dancing about with her money. Seems quite clear to me."

"I've killed no one," Bookman muttered and stared down at the gravel.

"Ha!" was Athelney Jones' only reply.

"It's that murder—and another probable— we must discuss," said Holmes.

The policeman's eyes widened. "Another murder you say?"

Holmes motioned for the detective to join him, and the two of them walked off together. As they moved away, I overheard Athelney Jones employ his favourite sobriquet for Holmes: "And what does 'The Theorist' have to say about this little matter?—two killed, no less."

To my surprise, however, it was Athelney Jones who did most of the talking, Holmes nodding as he took in the information. In one instance, my friend exclaimed, "Capital!" and toward the end of their conversation, on glancing at Bookman, he murmured, "As I expected."

Some ten minutes passed before the two detectives returned. When they did, Holmes addressed Hamlin Garland. "Please arrange for everyone to meet in the sitting room in the same manner we did last night. There is a new development to consider."

Only Lena and Lucille were missing from the group now milling about in front of the house, and Garland dutifully went off to find the pair. The others—Cedric, Owen, Charlotte and Mrs. Bookman—had heard Holmes' request. Amidst a buzz of nervous chatter and the occasional glance at the two policemen and their chained prisoner, everyone returned to the sitting room.

Garland retrieved the missing women, and we all took the same seats we had occupied the previous evening. Lena and Charlotte, the couch; Cedric, the wing chair; Garland and Lucille—once more with Oliver in her arms—the settee; and Owen, the wooden bow-back chair that stood where he had left it the night before. I resumed my place on the ottoman which I had rolled off to the side.

On this occasion, with her husband so obviously involved, Mrs. Bookman attended from the start, leaning against the wall near the archway to the dining room. For his part, the butler, still manacled and still gazing downward, was seated in another bow-back chair, his attendant constable standing behind him whilst keeping a cautious eye out for any more possible evil-doers. I am certain it did not help Bookman's piece of mind when Oliver's head perked up and the terrier started growling in the direction of the butler.

Holmes surprised me by commencing his remarks with a rare public compliment for one of the Yarders. "Let me begin," said he, "by thanking Inspector Athelney Jones for his determined investigative work."

The detective had been standing off to the side, and when Holmes called out the burly fellow, the inspector's face turned a florid colour and his chest seemed to swell with pride.

"Thanks to Scotland Yard," Holmes said, at the same time motioning for Athelney Jones to come forward and address the group, "we now know what Mr. Bookman was up to in London. Hear from the inspector himself the details he has uncovered."

With a broad grin, Athelney Jones paraded towards Holmes. So thoroughly did the inspector seem to relish his role that one felt like applauding. Holmes stepped away, and the inspector, now commanding the stage, withdrew a small notebook from a coat pocket and with dramatic slowness sought the relevant pages.

"Ha!" he emitted upon finding the passage he wanted. "It seems that your Mr. Norton Bookman here"—he flashed a thumb in the direction of the butler—"took the early train from Haslemere to London yesterday morning."

"London?" Mrs. Bookman queried.

"Aye," said Athelney Jones. "Waterloo Station, to be precise."

"You mean he didn't call upon the local constabulary as I requested?" asked Owen.

"No, he arrived at Waterloo. There he hired a hansom to transport him to St. Pancras where he purchased a ticket for the night-train to Dover. From Dover he planned to sail to France. Calais, actually."

"Leave me here, would you?" spat out Mrs. Bookman at her husband, a sneer mirroring her revulsion.

Bookman stared at the floor.

"On his way to St. Pancras," the inspector reported, "your butler stopped in a pub." Athelney Jones looked down at his notes to be certain he got the name right. "The Skinners Arms in Judd Street. Did some imbibing, he did, and at the same time started flashing a lot of fresh pound-notes."

Cedric and Owen glanced at each other. Like everyone else in the sitting room, I suspected that those bank notes had come from the desk of Mrs. Cobb.

"Fact is," Athelney Jones continued, "Mr. Bookman here was making such a loud show of his money that the publican became alarmed and sent the barmaid out to find the local constable."

"How foolish can a man be?" muttered Mrs. Bookman with a shake of her head.

"Whom did the lass find?" the inspector asked rhetorically. "Only one of London's finest, Police Constable Newman here." He identified the officer with another flick of his thumb. "P.C. Newman returned with the barmaid to the Skinners Arms and immediately started questioning Mr. Bookman. Your man said he worked as butler here at Hearthstone in Hindhead, he did. Described the money in his possession as his life savings, which he'd kept hidden in his cottage. Ha! P.C. Newman—clever fellow that he is—would have none of it. Brand-new bank-notes? They looked nothing at all like what one would have lying about for years."

"Most perceptive," observed my friend.

"Right you are, Mr. Holmes," replied Athelney Jones, beaming as if the compliment had been meant for himself instead of the constable.

Holmes leant over and whispered in my ear: "*L'amour-propre est le plus grand de tous les flatteurs.*"*

"Upon further questioning," the inspector went on, "your butler revealed that whilst in London, he often took his employer, Mrs. Muriel Cobb, to Holder and Stevenson, the bank in Threadneedle Street."

(I recognised the bank from a previous investigation almost a decade earlier. It was at that

---

* "Self-love is the greatest of flatterers." No. 2 of *Les Maximes* of Rochefoucauld. Athelney Jones evoked from Holmes a similar maxim from Rochefoucauld (No. 451) in *The Sign of Four*: "*Il n'y a pas des sots si incommodes que ceux qui ont de l'esprit.*" ("There are no fools so troublesome as those who have some wit.")

same private institution where the ill-fated Beryl Coronet had been placed as security for a loan.)

"That's right," said Owen. "I accompanied my mother there myself many times."

"At this point," Athelney Jones continued, "P.C. Newman became suspicious. Conveyed Bookman to Scotland Yard, he did. The case was assigned to me, don't you know, and, first thing, I checked the serial numbers of the bills he'd been waving about against the numbers Holder and Stevenson reported to us that they had recently paid out to Mrs. Cobb."

"Let me guess," Owen said. "A match."

"Ha!" exclaimed Athelney Jones. "Right you are, Mr. Cobb. Furthermore, when I searched Mr. Bookman, I found a bottle of pills." He held up the vial for all to see.

"May I?" I asked, extending my palm.

"Ah, yes, Dr. Watson." With a broad, self-satisfied grin, the inspector handed me the small bottle.

I removed the top and gingerly touched a pill to the tip of my tongue. Once more the bitter taste confirmed my suspicion. "Morphine," I said.

"Good, good," the inspector agreed. "The same conclusion as our chemist at the Yard." Turning to my friend, he said, "No need for theorizing this go-round, eh, Mr. Holmes? Bookman admitted to leaving a number of such pills in a bottle for Mrs. Cobb. The noose tightens."

It was Owen who put to Athelney Jones the question that was doubtless in everyone's mind: "Are you saying that Bookman killed our mother, Inspector?"

The detective's eyes dimmed a bit. "Well, no. Not yet. Bit of a mix-up, actually. Bookman told us he got the pills from the gamekeeper"—Athelney Jones consulted his notes again—"a Mr. Andrew Fairley—who, Mr. Holmes has just informed me, was himself found dead. Murdered, according to Mr. Holmes."

"But if Bookman's been in London all this time," Cedric said, "then he could not have killed Fairley."

"Quite so," Athelney Jones replied. He seemed rather deflated at having to confront so perplexing a new riddle.

"Well then, who did?" Charlotte demanded.

"Can't say just yet," answered Athelney Jones quietly.

Grumblings of disappointment arose in response.

Athelney Jones rubbed his hands together. I believe that by then he was more than prepared to end his current participation in the matter. Indeed, the inspector quickly announced, "I now call upon Mr. Holmes to explain the current affairs here at

Hearthstone—" Athelney Jones raised a hand as if to deflect any criticism—"about most of which, I must admit, I myself am only hearing for the first time."

Heads turned and followed Holmes as he made his way back to the front of the room.

Chapter Nine

Explanations

> Nearly all the popular successes of the last twenty years
> have been the result of pandering to this taste for the illicit.
> Stories which used to be confined to saloons and brothels
> are now printed in the regular book form
> and brought into the dining room.
> —Hamlin Garland
> Letter to Fred. B. Miller
> March 1, 1937

*O*nce again, Sherlock Holmes faced the group. "Many people in police work claim that they do not believe in coincidences. To them I say, 'What dull lives you must lead.' For though I tend to disregard the use of coincidence to explain the unexplainable, I also accept the fact that such situations do occur. As one did here at Hearthstone.

"The murder of Mrs. Cobb and the theft of her money are two separate crimes," my friend explained. "They were planned by two different individuals, the two plots coincidentally colliding in the murder of Andrew Fairley. Saturday night when Mrs. Cobb was killed—that is, the night of the storm—happened to be the same night that Bookman and Fairley had chosen in advance to steal Mrs. Cobb's money. Fairley's death is the key to understanding what happened that night."

"Explain," said Owen.

"Norton Bookman and Andrew Fairley agreed to steal the money they knew Mrs. Cobb kept locked in the drawer of her *escritoire*. As we have heard, Bookman confessed to leaving the morphine pills to render Mrs. Cobb unconscious. Earlier, he had doctored her bromide with green ink to force her to rely on the pills, which incidentally he had got from Fairley."

"Why did Fairley have the pills in the first place?" asked Charlotte.

"He was the gamekeeper, Charlotte," Owen said as slowly as if he were talking to a simpleton. "He used them to calm the horses when they required some sort of treatment."

"The thieves' next challenge," Holmes continued, "was getting into Mrs. Cobb's bedroom. In his travels through the house as butler, Bookman had left the sash window in her room unlatched. It was raining at the time, but not hard enough to dissuade them. After all, the morphine had already been planted.

"You all know the balcony outside Mrs. Cobb's window. It would require a ladder to reach it from the gardens. When Bookman reasoned she'd had enough time to lose consciousness, he retrieved a single-storey ladder from the tool shed and was about to set it up beneath the balcony. That was when the dog Oliver started to bark."

At the mention of his name, the terrier raised his head again.

At the same time, the butler, who continued looking at the floor during Holmes' account, began to squirm. Obviously, he knew what was coming next.

"To silence the dog," Holmes said, "Bookman hit the creature with some tool or other."

This time his name was mentioned, the terrier began barking at Bookman, and Lucille had to grasp him tightly.

Mrs. Bookman glared at her husband. "As much of a chance shutting the dog up," she observed, "as getting away with the money."

"In any case," continued Holmes, "Bookman climbed the ladder to the balcony, made his way into Mrs. Cobb's bedroom and, seeing the woman was lying insensate in her bed, concluded that the morphine had done its job. It was then child's play to steal the money. With a minimum of fuss, he broke open the drawer of the *escritoire* and collected her bank notes. He then retraced his steps, proceeding out the window to the balcony and down the ladder. After replacing the ladder in the tool shed, he returned to his cottage where Fairley was waiting to hear the results."

"And Mrs. Bookman didn't know?" Owen asked.

"No, Mr. Owen, I did *not*," answered Mrs. Bookman coldly. "You'll recall I'd left our cottage. I was in the house. All that drinking Fairley and Norton were doing. Mr. Cedric had been there earlier as well. I didn't want to be around them. Besides, I'd promised Miss Charlotte I'd help with her costumes, and that's what I did. I told you—I slept on the kitchen cot when we finished."

"Quite so," said Holmes. "Yet after Bookman secured the money, things didn't go as the thieves had planned. From the inspector, I learned that Bookman had wanted Fairley to go check that all was in order in the tool shed. But Fairley was too drunk to be of any assistance."

"Bloody fool," the butler muttered.

"Fairley complained about the rain. He complained about being told what to do. He complained so much that Bookman got disgusted with his erstwhile partner and decided to continue on his own."

"Double-crossed Fairley, you mean?" Garland said.

"Not to mention his wife," Mrs. Bookman added.

"Yes, exactly," said Holmes. "It was about then that Owen Cobb claimed to have discovered his mother's dead body. With a suspicion of foul play based on the tainted sleeping medication, he went pounding on the cottage door shouting at Bookman to go for the police in Haslemere. But, alas, unbeknownst to Owen, Bookman was already gone."

"That's right," Owen agreed.

"Hold on," said Cedric. "Owen told us he'd sent Bookman to bring the police here."

"Right," Owen said again. "I shouted at Bookman through the door. I told him to bring the authorities from Haslemere. Naturally, I thought he heard me and would carry on as I instructed."

Cedric shook his head at the answer.

"Bookman left," Holmes continued, "because he feared the theft of the money had been detected. Why else would someone be pounding on his door? He didn't wait round to hear Owen's orders to go for the police. Instead, he climbed out a back window and after making his escape across the rear portion of the estate, walked the short distance to Haslemere and boarded the train for London. Bookman knew nothing of Fairley's death and couldn't have been responsible for it. As Cedric has already pointed out, your butler was busy drinking in London at the time of the gamekeeper's murder."

"With our mother's money," Charlotte said.

"So," asked Garland, "who killed Fairley?"

Nervous eyes crisscrossed the room. No one spoke.

"In a moment," said Holmes. "As I explained last night, I examined Mrs. Cobb's armoire, the spot to which, as we already know, Lena Laughton hastened after the lightning had struck the oak tree. Upon examining the armoire, I discovered a narrow crack in the left-hand door. Admittedly, it is hard to notice because of the blackened wood-grain. Yet recall that the gas lamp by the bedside was lit—presumably, Mrs. Cobb had intended to read her Brontë novel—but the morphine took its toll. One would think that through the crack in the door of the armoire, Lena could easily see Mrs. Cobb in the illuminated room."

"No, no,' protested Lena. "I could see into the room, but I couldn't see my sister in the bed. The footboard is too high. I couldn't see poor Muriel, only everyone standing round her. It was from hearing what you all were saying at her bedside that I realised she must have died."

"So why didn't you show yourself, Aunt Lena?" Charlotte asked.

Lena's face coloured. "Remaining hidden seemed the only practical decision, dear. I was too ashamed to be found out. Even though I discovered that Muriel's money had already been stolen, I've admitted to you previously that I'd gone in there to take it. I couldn't show myself."

Charlotte put her arm round her aunt's shoulders.

Lena raised a hand to her mouth to stifle a sob. "How was I to know," she managed to say, "that Owen would lock the door, trapping me inside the room? I only pretended to be shocked when he told me Muriel had died."

"Indeed," said Holmes. "But the locking of the door is not the salient feature of Miss Laughton's account. We must not overlook its most significant detail. Recall that though she couldn't see the body itself, she could nonetheless see the people in the room standing round the bed. What follows then is the crucial question that establishes the identity of the killer: did Miss Laughton see anyone enter her sister's bedroom *before* the rest of you came in to pay your respects? I ask you directly, Miss Laughton. Did you see anyone at all who might have come in and stood by the side of the bed?

"No, I did not," Lena said.

It was Hamlin Garland who provided the logic behind Holmes' question. "Owen came downstairs to tell us that his mother was dead. He said he had checked her pulse."

"Precisely the point," said Sherlock Holmes. "I submit to you, ladies and gentlemen, that there were only two ways Owen Cobb could have known his mother was dead. The most benign explanation would be that he entered the room and discovered her body."

"But," Garland was quick to point out, "Lena Laughton has already told us that that did not happen, that she saw no one enter the room before all the rest of us did."

"Quite so," said Holmes.

A furrow crossed Cedric's brow. "So, what was the other way Owen could have known his mother was dead?"

"What do you think, brother?" Charlotte replied sarcastically.

Garland spoke up again. "The killer would know. Owen would have had no need to go back into her room to confirm his mother's death if he himself was responsible for murdering her."

"Precisely," said Holmes.

Strange to say, the conversation had continued as if Owen himself were not present among us. For his part, with but a self-conscious smile, he listened quite calmly to the accusatory remarks.

"I suggest," Holmes concluded, "that before Lena Laughton entered her sister's room to steal the money, Owen Cobb had preceded her. Discovering his mother to be in a morphine-induced sleep, he recognised the situation to be the perfect opportunity to become master of Hearthstone Hall. In a word, he strangled his own mother."

No one spoke. Instead, everyone in the sitting room looked to Owen for an explanation.

Chapter Ten

Resolution

> You see, I studied baseball pitching,
> and I know the action of a whirling sphere . . . .
> I can make it do all kinds of "stunts."
> —Hamlin Garland
> *Victor Ollnee's Discipline*

*W*ith all eyes upon him, the freshly crowned lord of the manor slipped his hand into a side pocket of his aptly-named shooting jacket and withdrew a slate-grey revolver, a Webley Mark Three as best I could discern.

"He has a gun!" screamed one of the female voices.

Oliver began to bark.

"Owen," shouted Cedric, "what are you doing?"

Actually, it was quite clear what he was doing. Sweeping the barrel of the revolver in the general direction of the rest of us, he was backing his way towards the front door. Only for a moment did he pause to aim the gun directly at Holmes. "Very clever, Sherlock Holmes. Very clever, indeed."

"Don't make it any worse for yourself," Athelney Jones pleaded.

But Owen glared at all the faces now staring at him. "I killed Mother to gain my inheritance. Isn't it obvious? *Cui bono?*"

"Owen!" Lucille exclaimed. "What are you saying?"

"What about Mother's ring, brother?" Charlotte demanded. "How did it end up in Cedric's trunk?"

Owen responded with a grotesque grin. "A fair question, I suppose, considering we're all family. I went to Bookman's cottage to get him to fetch the police, just as I said. What better way to be considered innocent than appearing desirous of having the authorities come investigate? But when I got no response banging on Bookman's door, I reckoned I could tell you all I sent him for the police and frame *him* for Mother's murder at the same time."

Bookman sneered at Owen's underhanded plot, but the man with the gun ignored him and continued his confession. "I opened the cottage door with my master key and hid the ring under the cushion of Bookman's couch. Much to my sorrow, I didn't realise that a drunk Fairley, who was somewhere in the far reaches of the cottage, saw where I had stashed it. Soon after I left, he grabbed it for himself.

"Fairley found me later in the day. He told me it would be worth my while to meet him in secret at Demon's Drop within the hour. It was still raining at the appointed time though not very hard, and I grabbed the first jacket I saw hanging near the door—yours, Cedric, as it so happened.

"I climbed the wooden stile and found Fairley pacing back and forth not far from the edge of the Drop. When I reached him, he had the audacity to try to blackmail me.

"'I figger it worth, say, a thousand pounds, to keep m'mouth shut about this ring,' he said.

"Well, I would have none of it. I motioned him closer. I said, 'Let me see the ring so I can be sure it's the real thing.' The fool held it out in his palm, and when he did, I snatched it, gave the fellow a push, and over the edge he went. As soon as I got back to the house, I hid the ring in Cedric's trunk. When I learned that Fairley had torn off one of your coat buttons, brother, I reckoned that bit of evidence would solidify your guilt and leave me in the clear."

Cedric narrowed his venomous eyes and muttered some hateful oath.

"Alas," sighed Owen, "thanks to Mr. Holmes here, all my careful planning turned out to be for naught."

Athelney Jones tried reasoning. "Mr. Cobb, it's time to put down the gun. You—"

Oliver began barking again, but Oliver was Owen's dog as well as Lucille's.

"Quiet, boy," Owen said gently whilst still waving the Webley—now at Athelney Jones—and the dog settled down.

"No, Inspector," said Owen, "you're wrong. It's not time to put away the pistol; rather, it's time to make my escape." With those words, he turned about sharply, dashed through the outer doorway, and slammed the door shut behind him.

By the time P.C. Newman shoved it open and took up the chase, we could see Owen heading across the gravel towards the railed fence near Devil's Drop and the dusty paths and isolated trails leading into the Punch Bowl—in short, an abundance of escape routes. If he made it over the rim, he could find numerous places to hide among the brush and trees that covered most of the moor.

At the same time, Hamlin Garland sprinted towards his valise in the entry hall. In one singular motion, he cracked open the top, yanked out Conan Doyle's cherry-red cricket ball, and darted out onto the stone porch.

With his sharp eyes on the target, he calculated for a fraction of a second, wound up and, emitting a decidedly loud grunt, whipped his arm down, letting loose one of his swiftest pitches. The ball flew straight and true, a crimson blur as it traversed the landscape, and struck the fleeing Owen

Cobb hard in the centre of his back. The gun flew from his hand as down he tumbled, his face crunching into the hard gravel beneath him.

That blow was all Constable Newman required to catch up to his prey. In the next moment, the policeman sprang at Owen who lay sprawled on his stomach. Landing on Owen's back, Newman secured the man's wrists behind him with the policeman's darbies, the solid click of the manacles offering welcome assurance.

Athelney Jones moved towards the prostrate figures with surprising speed for so stout a man. However winded, he stooped to pick up the errant revolver and placed it carefully in his pocket. Slowly, he approached the struggling captive, looked down, and addressed him.

"Mr. Owen Lester Cobb," wheezed Athelney Jones, "I am arresting you in the name of the Queen for the murders of Muriel Cobb and Andrew Fairley. You need not say anything, but if you do, whatever you say may be used against you in criminal court."

P.C. Newman got to his feet, and gripping Owen under the arms, jerked the confessed killer upright. One hesitates to repeat the imprecations hurled at Owen by his brother Cedric, but the tears shed by his sister Charlotte and his Aunt Lena that forenoon most certainly revealed the depths of feeling the dramatic developments of the morning had elicited.

A solitary crow circled over the scene. Apparently finding nothing of interest, it flew off over the desolate moor.

Chapter Eleven

Baker Street Again

Definition of Break *(in cricket):*
Verb: said of a ball: to change direction on hitting the ground
Noun: the deviation of a ball on striking the pitch
—*Chambers English Dictionary*

"Matricide," Hamlin Garlin ruminated over his glass of port. "It's mythological in its proportions."

"Most disturbing indeed," I said.

Holmes and I were taking refreshment with the American in our Baker Street sitting room. Once Athelney Jones and Constable Newman had left the manor house with prisoners Cobb and Bookman, we joined Garland in offering our own farewells to the remaining members of the Cobb family, and the three of us returned by train to London.

Garland stared into his ruby-coloured wine. Clearly, it would require more than a few swallows to compensate for the disturbing knowledge he had gained about his former friend, Owen Cobb. "What human passions can prompt men to do," he philosophised with a slow shake of his head. "You do know," he persisted, "that the Greeks considered matricide among the most offensive crimes to the gods."

"With good cause," Holmes said.

"Was it not Orestes," I remembered, "who murdered his mother Clytemnestra?"

"Quite so, Watson," Holmes replied, gently waving his glass to underscore his point, "but unlike Orestes, who was pardoned by Athena for his crime, I'm bound to say that no such figure will come to the defence of Owen Cobb."

"We should have known," I said to Holmes. "Owen told us so himself. *Cui bono?*"

"Quite so," Holmes said again, "but when regarded objectively, each one of the possible suspects—the Cobb children and the servants—stood to gain from the death of Muriel Cobb. All would have benefitted—at least, from the earlier will."

"Agreed," said Garland. "Each one had good reason to wish her dead, but only Owen had the cold-heartedness to commit such an act."

"Very true," observed my friend. "It is ever thus in life. Imagine how many murders would take place if the majority of men possessed as cold a heart as Owen Cobb."

"Women too," I added.

"Still," said Holmes, "the truth of the matter remains—in establishing Owen as her lone beneficiary, Mrs. Cobb might just as well have signed a warrant for her own death. Immediately after learning of her decision to elevate his inheritance, Owen Cobb concluded that it would be to his great advantage to have his mother out of the way."

Hamlin Garland sighed and sampled his drink once more. "I believe I've had my fill of all this talk of matricide. Such horror was not what drew me to England. Might we turn our attention to lighter matters?"

Sherlock Holmes raised his long index finger. "I have just the thing," he smiled, "a more uplifting coincidence than the dire circumstance at Hearthstone Hall." Holmes set aside his glass and turned to me. "Do you recall, Watson, that we concluded our Baskerville investigation with a musical distraction?"

I had to think for a moment. Holmes was asking me to remember events from a decade earlier. But eventually it came to me. "Now that you mention it," I said, "I do recollect it. With the intention of putting the more diabolical aspects of the case out of mind, you asked me if I had ever heard the De Reskes sing. When I replied in the negative, you insisted I accompany you to their performance in *Les Huguenots.*"

"The opera by Meyerbeer," Garland offered.

"That's the one," I said. "Quite the stirring performance. We sat in a box near the stage, if memory serves."

"Indeed, we did," Holmes smiled. "Well, in a most singular coincidence, at the same time we find ourselves at the conclusion of another disturbing case, the brothers De Reske—Jean the tenor and Edouard the bass—are once more here in London and performing this very evening. I suggest a night full of music to be just the tonic for putting out of mind any further thoughts of the havoc that took place at Hearthstone Hall."

"Dinner at Marcini's again?" I suggested.

Garland stroked his beard. "Sounds like just the thing to me. I've always been attracted to the higher qualities of musical art."

Within minutes the three of us were climbing into a cab for Covent Garden.*

---

* In another coincidence that none of the three music-enthusiasts could have predicted, twenty-seven years later, a student of Jean de Reszke, a tenor named Hardesty Johnson, (considered by Jean to be the "ideal" Lohengrin) would become the first husband of Isabel Garland, Hamlin Garland's older daughter. The couple divorced in 1936, and Isabel went on to marry Mindret Lord, whose own first wife had harbored a romantic interest in Hardesty when, in a second coincidence, she too had been a student of de Reszke in Nice.

As a kind of *dénouement*, I offer the following details. In the mid-summer following the grim events that had taken place at Hearthstone Hall, Owen Cobb was found guilty of killing both his mother and the gamekeeper and condemned to death. Besides the requirements of a legal defence, no one, not a single family member, came to the Old Bailey to support him. Once the mandated wait for three-Sundays-following-sentence had passed, the erstwhile poet, Owen Lester Cobb, was hanged at Wandsworth Prison.

Sherlock Holmes proved quite prescient in recognizing that everyone at Hearthstone stood to profit from Mrs. Cobb's death. Given the murderous exploits of Muriel Cobb's solitary heir, Ebenezer Falwell, the solicitor who had drawn up her prior will, managed a kind of reversion to its original conditions, and Cedric, Charlotte, and Lena inherited the shares previously designated to them by Mrs. Cobb. Charlotte used her money to resume her dancing career. Lena invested hers to establish a household with her friend in Blackpool. And Cedric, the new lord of Hearthstone, announced his plans to modernise the place.

"New furniture might be nice," he reportedly said, "and I hear that electricity is predicted to have a successful future—more so than drinking."

For the theft of his employer's money, butler Norton Bookman was incarcerated at

Wandsworth where he might still be imprisoned today. His wife Charity, choosing not to remain at Hearthstone, took the small inheritance Mrs. Cobb had originally bequeathed to the Bookmans and moved to Manchester to live with her sister. Lucille returned to Chicago with her terrier Oliver where, among her other desires, she intended to resume her friendship with Zulime Taft.

About Hamlin Garland, I may be more precise, for he sent me a letter just before Christmas that detailed his current affairs.

Dear Dr. Watson [it ran],

I write to you, author to author, with the hope that you will convey the contents of this letter to Sherlock Holmes. I feel it is only fitting to complete our work together with news of my immediate future, and yet I apologize for the long delay in communicating with you. As you shall learn, there have been a lot of distractions.

You see, Lucille Cobb was quite right in telling me how the brother of the woman I hoped to marry was twisting the truth when he said his sister was engaged to someone else. As soon as I confirmed this fact, I made my intentions known to Zulime. I asked her to come and starve and suffer with me, and I am pleased to say, that with some coaxing from L., she tolerated my suit, and eventually accepted it.

To make the proverbial long story short, we were married this past November 18. I confess to rushing the ceremony so we could honeymoon in the High Country and return in time to spend Thanksgiving at the homestead with the old folks—that is, my mother and father. We were married by a judge—Z.'s sufficiently liberal on such matters and not tied to religious ritual.

Afterwards, we travelled to Colorado though I think that during our Mountain West adventure I was more enamored with the horses than was my bride. Z. is a refined and dignified city-girl, and I'm afraid it will take some adjusting for her to live comfortably with a "son of the middle border" like myself—pleasant *adjusting, I should add, for I predict a long life together for the two of us and, as I fully expect, for our children as well. After all, now that my mother has gotten that daughter, she demands a grandchild.*

As you know, writing is not the most lucrative of professions, but speechifying adds to my earnings, and I believe that all should be fine. In any case, you may rest assured that, though I shall make no public reference to our distressing adventure at Hearthstone Hall, I surprise myself at the exhilaration I continue to feel when recalling the time that the three of us spent together in solving the mystery of Mrs. Cobb's murder.

In that spirit, I wish you and Mr. Holmes the happiest of holidays.

Hamlin Garland

With so strong a predilection for writing autobiographical narratives, it was rather remarkable to learn that Garland had decided not to publicise his involvement in the macabre events of 1899 in England. To be sure, he recorded his visits with personages like Arthur Conan Doyle, George Bernard Shaw, James Barrie, and Thomas Hardy (not to mention his fellow countrymen, Mark Twain and Bret Harte), but upon the passions that led to thievery and murder in the Surrey manor house he remained silent. For that matter, though the novel Garland completed the year after his trip tells of a cowboy who, like Garland himself, sails to these islands for the first time, *Her Mountain Lover* offers not even a hint of Garland's experience at Hearthstone.

What is more, even as the decades have slipped by, Garland has remained true to his pledge of silence. In perusing his publications of the past few years—including *A Daughter of the Middle Border,* winner of the Pulitzer Prize for biography in 1922—neither Holmes nor I have discovered any mention of Garland's role in solving the Hearthstone Hall murders. For that matter, not for my own lack of trying, I also do not believe he has ever boasted in public about the accuracy of his throwing arm—at least, not in print.

THE END

Editor's Notes

As she suggested in her letter to Sherlock Holmes, Isabel Garland Lord, Hamlin Garland's older daughter, did, in fact, dramatize in her novel, *Abandon Hope* (Arcadia House, 1941), the events reported by Watson. True to her word, she employed alternative venues, various aliases, and the occasional distorted action in order to maintain her father's privacy.

For additional details concerning Garland's 1899 meetings in England with such literary figures as Arthur Conan Doyle and George Bernard Shaw, see Garland's collection of essays titled *Roadside Meetings* published in 1930 with "decorations" by his younger daughter, Constance Garland. A number of additional accounts appear in *Hamlin Garland's Diaries* edited by Donald Piser. (It may also be noted that in his later years, Garland, like Conan Doyle, pursued an interest in the spiritual world.)

For more on the life of Hamlin Garland, readers may consult his autobiographical *A Son of the Middle Border* and, as Watson pointed out, its Pulitzer-

Prize-winning sequel, *A Daughter of the Middle Border*. It is recommended, however, that readers keep in mind the answer of Garland's wife Zulime to their daughter Isabel's question as to why Zulime hadn't read the latter, a biography of herself, after all: "Because it isn't true," Zulime replied.

For another perspective on the author, see Isabel Garland Lord's *A Summer to Be: A Memoir by the Daughter of Hamlin Garland*. Interestingly, as octogenarians, Isabel and her younger sister Constance spent the final years of their lives together, including a shared hospital room in Sherman Oaks, California, where both of them died within a few days of each other.

The fascinating story of the two sisters is told by Victoria Doyle-Jones, Constance's daughter, in her foreword to *A Summer to Be*. As tantalizing as the "Doyle" in Victoria's name may be in a narrative involving Sherlock Holmes, her father was Canadian by birth and seems unrelated to the family of Arthur Conan Doyle. Further study is encouraged.

For a more objective biography of Hamlin Garland, see Keith Newlin's *Hamlin Garland: A Life*. Readers may be fascinated to learn how an author like Garland, so deeply identifiable with the Midwest, spent the latter part of his life in Hollywood coping with various social entanglements involving his daughters and such figures as members of movie director Cecil B. DeMille's family and the surviving husband of aviator Amelia Earhart.

(It should be noted that, consistent with Garland's own silence on the murders at Hearthstone Hall during his 1899 trip to England, neither Newlin's biography nor Isabel Lord's memoir makes any mention of the crimes.)

For a discussion of the literary implications of Garland's 1899 trip to England, see "The Significance of Hamlin Garland's First Visit to England" by John R. Dove in *The University of Texas Studies in English* (1953).

Of related interest to readers of *The Hearthstone Manuscript* is *The Broom-Squire* by Sabine Baring-Gould, an intriguing novel set primarily in the Devil's Punch Bowl. Baring-Gould is the grandfather of Sherlock Holmes biographer and scholar, William S. Baring-Gould, who noted parallels between the childhoods of his grandfather Sabine and Sherlock Holmes. It should also be noted that Sabine Baring-Gould worked to preserve the prehistorical sites of Dartmoor, the setting for much of *The Hound of the Baskervilles*.

Finally, in *The Moor*, a fictional treatment of Holmes' adventures that takes him and his wife, Mary Russell, to Baskerville Hall, author Laurie R. King identifies Sabine Baring-Gould as the godfather of Sherlock Holmes.

Milton Keynes UK
Ingram Content Group UK Ltd.
UKHW031948281024
450365UK00008B/461

9 781804 244623